"Tanner? Tanner Davenport? What are you doing here?"

Charity MacKay. He might have been in Alaska for the past seven years, but he'd recognize that red hair flying in the breeze anywhere, and nobody sat a horse like Charity. Hoofbeats thundered as she reined in beside him and peered down as if he were an infestation of locusts.

"It's so *'you'* to drop out of the sky like some meteor and scare the bejeebers out of my horses," she quickly added.

He leaned against the Cessna, letting the April sun warm his bones, something he sure as hell couldn't do in Alaska this time of year. "Sorry about the horses, but I was low on gas."

"Since your farm is just over the next rise and twice as big as this place ever was, why aren't you scaring your own horses?"

"I really was low on gas. Besides, I saw you riding out, and we need to talk."

Charity slid to the ground and touched the plane as if it would bite. "I know diddly about Alaska. Figure if people were meant to fly we'd all have wings, and horses never were your strong suit. That makes for a real short conversation." She eyed him. "Why *are* you here?"

"The wedding? Your sister, my brother?" He shook his head. "I need to do something about it…"

Dear Reader,

I live in Cincinnati, and whenever I drive south I pass through a lot of orange barrels and bumper-to-bumper traffic and finally cross the Ohio River into the beautiful state of Kentucky.

Wild honeysuckle cascading across acres of zigzagging fences, hills of bluegrass rolling on for miles, hawks soaring overhead, Thoroughbred horses grazing in lush pastures, recipes for melt-in-your-mouth corn bread and white-lightning moonshine give Kentucky a unique flavor all its own.

I've always wanted to write a story about the horse farms and the owners who work relentlessly to keep them so perfect. *The Wedding Rescue* is that book.

I hope you enjoy reading about Tanner and Charity and their families and Kentucky. I'd love hearing from you at DianneCastell@hotmail.com. Let me know what's special about your neck of the woods.

Have fun!

Dianne Castell

Books by Dianne Castell

HARLEQUIN AMERICAN ROMANCE
888—COURT-APPOINTED MARRIAGE
968—HIGH-TIDE BRIDE

THE WEDDING RESCUE
Dianne Castell

TORONTO • NEW YORK • LONDON
AMSTERDAM • PARIS • SYDNEY • HAMBURG
STOCKHOLM • ATHENS • TOKYO • MILAN • MADRID
PRAGUE • WARSAW • BUDAPEST • AUCKLAND

ISBN 0-373-75011-0

THE WEDDING RESCUE

Copyright © 2004 by Dianne Kruetzkamp.

All rights reserved. Except for use in any review, the reproduction or
utilization of this work in whole or in part in any form by any electronic,
mechanical or other means, now known or hereafter invented, including
xerography, photocopying and recording, or in any information storage
or retrieval system, is forbidden without the written permission of the
publisher, Harlequin Enterprises Limited, 225 Duncan Mill Road,
Don Mills, Ontario, Canada M3B 3K9.

All characters in this book have no existence outside the imagination of
the author and have no relation whatsoever to anyone bearing the same
name or names. They are not even distantly inspired by any individual
known or unknown to the author, and all incidents are pure invention.

This edition published by arrangement with Harlequin Books S.A.

® and TM are trademarks of the publisher. Trademarks indicated with
® are registered in the United States Patent and Trademark Office, the
Canadian Trade Marks Office and in other countries.

Visit us at www.eHarlequin.com

Printed in U.S.A.

To Lori Foster, wonderful friend and fantastic author.
Thanks for everything.

To Susan Litman, for your help,
guidance, encouragement and friendship.

Chapter One

The Cessna coughed, then sputtered. Fuel? Tanner Davenport glanced at his instrument panel. *Hell.* He was almost out, and that was damn inconvenient since he was two hundred feet above ground. He should have topped off his tanks, but getting home to his big brother's doomed wedding made him push the limit. That limit was fast approaching.

Treetops gave way to lush spring grass glistening with morning dew. Grazing horses scattered in all directions. "Sorry guys," he muttered.

He spotted a lone rider as he leveled off, adjusted flaps and grit his teeth as the wheels touched ground, jarring him like an egg dropped from a tall chicken. Now if only he didn't crack like one. He applied brakes, stopping just short of the brown split-rail fence. Was he a good bush pilot or what? More like a damn lucky one...and damn stupid for getting so low on fuel in the first place.

He pushed open the door, stepped down and ritually kissed his fingers and touched the wing for luck. Today he touched it twice. He took a KitKat from his pocket, peeled back the red wrapper and chomped into it as a warm breeze kissed his cheek. Wild honeysuckle cascaded across acres of zigzagging fences, hills rolled on as far as he could see and hawks soared overhead. Bluegrass Ridge, Kentucky. Home…for better and worse. And right now a touch of the better came his way at full gallop.

Charity MacKay. He might have been in Alaska for the past seven years, but he'd recognize that red hair flying in the breeze anywhere, and nobody sat a horse like Charity. Hoofbeats thundered until she reined in her fine-looking Morgan beside him and peered down as if he were an infestation of locusts. Her eyes suddenly lit with recognition.

"Tanner? Tanner Davenport? What in the Sam Hill are you doing here?" A little smile tipped her lips…her soft pink lips? "Though it's so *you* to drop out of the sky like some meteor and scare the bejeebers out of my horses."

He leaned against the Cessna, letting the April sun warm his bones, something he sure as hell couldn't do in Alaska this time of year. Then Charity smiled, warming him even more. How'd that happen? *Why'd* that happen? "Sorry about the horses, but I was low on gas."

"If I remember correctly, your excuses for mayhem used to be a lot more creative. Since Thistledown is just over the next rise and your farm is twice as big as this place ever was, why aren't you scaring your own horses?"

"Not *my* place or *my* horses. And I was *really* low on gas." He gave her an easy smile. "Besides, I saw you out riding and we need to talk."

Charity slid to the ground and touched the plane as if it would bite. "I know diddly about Alaska. Figure if people were meant to fly we'd all have wings, and horses were never your strong suit. That makes for a real short conversation." She looked back to him. "Why *are* you here?"

"The wedding? Your sister, my brother?" He shook his head. "I need to do something about it."

Her green eyes danced. Charity MacKay never had wonderful green eyes before, had she?

"You came in early to find the perfect wedding gift? I know what you mean, it'll be a challenge to come up with something unique since Nathan already has the perfect house and the perfect horse farm. Now he'll have the perfect wife."

"You think so?"

"Oh, my, yes. You must be thrilled Nathan and Savannah are tying the knot. You two were good friends. Think I saw more of you at our kitchen table than her. Nathan wants the wedding at Thistledown, he's even bringing up a chef from New Orleans to cater. He and Savannah handpicked the orchids for the bouquets and table settings."

"A two-month engagement seems a little on the fast side."

"Nathan and Savannah have known each other since birth. Nothing fast about that."

He stroked the filly nuzzling Charity's shoulder, then stepped around her and swung himself into the saddle with an ease he hadn't forgotten. That surprised him. It was a long time since he'd been on horseback. A long time since he wanted to be. Brought back one hell of a lot of memories. His smile slipped a notch.

Charity put her hands to her hips, firm and slender from years of riding. "Are you all comfy up there on *my* horse?"

"I need fuel for the Cessna, but I'm willing to share…" He arched his brow in question, waiting for her to supply the name.

"Ranger."

He laughed. "A filly named Ranger? Couldn't you go for Princess or Fluffy?"

Her lips curved into an inviting smile as sunlight played on her red hair, turning it to fire. "Still getting your own way and calling the shots."

He laughed again, stroked Ranger and ignored the smile and fire. "That's the one area where you and I are tied dead-even."

He shed his leather jacket and looped it over the saddle, then held out his hand to help her up. "Come on, Kentucky Girl, it's a long walk back. I'll give you a ride.''

''My, my. Chivalry is not dead after all.''

She grabbed his hand and he nearly dropped her. He hadn't expected touching Charity MacKay to be so…so…intense? She'd never been intense before. She'd been a blur, the oldest of three sisters, the worker bee, the serious one who held MacKay Farms together on a shoestring.

A breeze molded her white cotton blouse to her rounded breasts and he did a mental head shake. Hips? Breasts? Lips? Not a blur anywhere.

''Is there a problem?''

Damn good question. ''Been a while since I've ridden.''

She nodded at Ranger's tail. ''Back.'' She nodded toward the head. ''Front. That's the part you steer.''

''I've been welcomed home by a smart aleck.''

''What happened to Kentucky Girl?''

That's what I want to know. She slid up behind him and wrapped her arms around his middle as he nudged Ranger into a walk. ''So, you really do think this marriage is a good idea?''

''Good? Flyboy, this wedding left *good* behind weeks ago. Wait till you see Savannah's dress. It's a Vera Wang.''

''I don't remember a Vera on the Ridge. She made Savannah's dress?''

''This is the reason men are not allowed to plan

weddings. Savannah's colors are weeping willow and peach blossom. There are eight bridesmaids, and white rose petals in the aisle. They had an engagement party at the Horseman's Club. We gave up our membership some years ago but Nathan's connected.''

''You're sure excited enough about this wedding. If I didn't know better, I'd think you were the one getting married.''

''Me?'' Her warm hands resting on his middle, her slender arms around his sides and her front that grazed his back stiffened. Then *he* stiffened, lest the portion below his belt did.

''Hardly. I'm…I'm just happy Savannah's getting the wedding and the man of her dreams.''

''Nate's the best, that's for sure.'' Charity's legs brushed his, making him more aware of her than before…*as if that were possible.*

Okay, enough. What the hell was going on? Why was he behaving like a complete dolt? He and Charity were never close. She was like…*his* big sister as well as Savannah's. Was Charity three or four years his senior? *Who cared!* But his hormonal surge did not suggest *sister* at all—that much he felt sure of. Maybe this awareness came from there being ten males for every one woman in Alaska. Yeah, that must be it. Her touch felt warm, gentle, feminine—he could tell right through his shirt. The surge kicked up a notch and he squirmed.

"What's wrong now?"

"Nothing." *Everything.* "How far away is that house of yours? Did you move it?"

"Put it on roller skates and slid it down the lane. Piece of cake. You sure you didn't knock your head when you landed back there?"

Home. He had to make it there and to get both of them off this horse. He nudged Ranger into a trot. Charity's hands gripped tighter, her chest rubbing in a steady rhythm. His condition did not improve one iota.

The farm came into view. *'Bout damn time.* He had to think of something other than the woman behind him. *Good luck.* "Nice buns. Uh, b*arns.* I mean, barns." His brain had turned to mush.

He looked around, desperate for distraction. The roof on the house was shot and the cars old. He pulled up and she dismounted. He stayed put, leaning forward slightly to conceal his aroused state. How embarrassing was this? He couldn't even get off the damn horse without advertising he was one horny Alaskan. He hadn't hit his head in that emergency landing, but it had sure jarred his hormones.

CHARITY STUDIED TANNER. He wore a soft denim shirt and he smelled of fresh winds and tall pines. That, mixed with the heat of his skin seeping into her as they rode back, had made for a long, unsettling trip. Trouble was, she still felt unsettled. This was not the same twenty-one-year-old who had left the Ridge eight years ago. He'd grown up. A lot.

She ran her fingers through her hair, lifting it off her neck, taking in Tanner's fine brown eyes and thick lashes. Mercy, it sure was hot for April. "Savannah and Nathan really seem happy. I'm sure you realized that from just talking to Nathan."

Tanner gazed her way looking…pained? Maybe from the rough landing. "My brother's been so preoccupied with breeding and training race horses for the past ten years, anyone would look good to him."

"Savannah's not just anyone. She *was* Miss Bluegrass two years in a row and had every male on the Ridge in love with her at one time or another. You must remember. Seven years and ten and a half months isn't *that* long ago."

"You've kept track?"

Heat rushed to her face. "Uh…sure. Heck, everybody has. Marked it off on the calendar in big Xs. Been reveling in the peace and quiet. No more biplane doing loopy things over our pastures. No more fast cars tearing up our gravel driveways. No more skinny-dipping in Blue Stone Pond."

Whoops. Tanner's eyes widened as if surprised she knew about such a thing. She knew. Oh, Lordy, did she. Once, looking for Savannah at the pond, she'd seen Tanner get out of the water, alone, dripping wet. In the full moonlight, she'd glimpsed his muscles and nice butt. *Great butt.* "How…how do you like Alaska?"

"It's far away from the Ridge."

"Is that a good or a bad thing? Do you miss it?"

"It's necessary." He shrugged. "I miss Nate a hell of a lot. And I miss your mama's fried chicken and corn bread."

He grinned. Did he have to grin? He had a great grin, almost as good as his… *Heavenly days,* the man was an eyeful coming and going. Snagging his jacket, he hooked his leg over the saddle and slid to the ground. A breeze ruffled his chestnut hair, sending a lock over his forehead as he handed Ranger off to one of the high school kids who worked part-time around the stables.

Tanner gave Charity a long, searching look. Oh, no. He knew about the pond. She was sure he did. He'd seen her and—

"Doesn't this wedding bother you just a little?"

Glory be, he was back to the wedding again. No pond, no Peeping Charity. Life was good. "Well, the wedding is expensive, but we'll manage. Nathan's paying for the reception and—"

"Not that." Tanner folded his arms. "Nathan's shy, works like a dog. If the housekeeper didn't keep his clothes organized and cut his hair, he'd look like Einstein. Savannah's…well, Savannah's the Ridge's answer to *Vogue* and *Cosmo* all rolled into one."

"That makes them the perfect match. They complement each other and bring out the best in each other.'' She nodded at the older-than-dirt pickup parked by the garage. ''Gas cans are next to the pump around back. Take what you need for the plane. I'm sure Puck won't mind riding with you, then he can drive the truck back.''

''Does he still have that apartment over your garage?''

''Yep, thank heaven. Don't know how we would have gotten by without him to help out around here all these years.''

She watched Tanner head off toward the storage tank and called, ''Hey, I forgot to give you suggestions for a wedding gift. That's what you wanted to talk about in the first place, wasn't it?''

He paused for a moment, then said, ''I'll think of something.'' He gave her a little salute. ''See you later.''

She turned for the house as the whinny of horses mixed with birdsong and the hum of insects. She took the stone path bordered with rosemary and lavender. Sprigs of peppermint trailed across the rocks, scenting the air as her boots crushed the leaves. Mama Kay's Welcome mat.

If she could *ever* save any money, she'd buy Mama a watering system. Maybe this year…if all went as planned, for a change. She ran her hand over her face and let out a long, deep sigh to ease the knot in her gut. She pulled a mint from her pocket, peeled back the wrapper and popped the disk in her mouth. Her stomach settled a bit as she opened the door to the screened-in porch and ducked under the patchwork canopy of green, yellow, blue and gray herbs hung upside-down to dry. She kissed her mother on the cheek, hugging her from behind as she repotted new thyme with expert care.

Charity plopped down into a wicker rocker and hitched her leg over one arm. "Why couldn't Tanner Davenport stay in Alaska where he belongs? Why couldn't he just FedEx Nathan and Savannah some moose antlers and smoked salmon as a wedding present?"

Her mother smiled as she reached for another pot. "I'm guessing that gibberish means Tanner's back on the Ridge, and since he was born and raised a mile down the road, he belongs here as much as you do. Not to mention that his only brother is getting married in two weeks." Mama stopped potting and gazed at Charity. "You don't sound too thrilled to see Tanner. Something wrong?"

Virile, rugged, handsome, muscular...great behind. "I wouldn't go straight to wrong, more like... agitating. Why he ever left one of the finest horse farms east of the Mississippi in the first place to go off and live with bears and seals is one of life's great mysteries. Don't you think?"

Mama's smile widened as she filled the pot with soil. "I know it's hard to believe, dear, but Thoroughbreds thundering across the finish line isn't everyone's dream.'' Her expression became more serious as she added, ''Something his daddy didn't understand one bit. Must have been hard for Tanner to come back. It would dredge up a lot of old memories.''

Charity admired her mother's perfect makeup that never looked made-up, her golden hair with fine streaks of silver that were more attractive than aging and pin-neat, crisp, blue blouse and floral skirt. *All right.* How did she do it? How could someone be up to their elbows in dirt and not get dirty? As Charity studied her own dusty jeans and smudged T-shirt, she realized she didn't have a clue. ''Well, he needs a shave, his hair's too long, that jacket he wears looks like a moose hibernated in it.''

''Moose don't hibernate, dear.''

''This one did.'' She sat upright and sighed. ''Tanner's not the same guy who left here, Mama. Not at all. He's…he's a *man.*''

Mama laughed, then winked. ''Do tell.''

''A sassy mother in the house. Just what every daughter needs.''

''After listening to three daughters carry on all these years, I figure it's my turn and then some.''

Bride-to-be Savannah breezed out from the kitchen, refreshing as a glass of iced tea on a scorching summer day. A cookie-cutter image of Mama.

''You wouldn't believe who dropped into town.

Tanner. I was on the phone with Nathan when he noticed his plane landing over at Thistledown. His very own bush plane all the way from Alaska.''

Charity sniffed a sprig of dried lavender. ''It's a Cessna. They're everywhere.''

''You don't understand because you hate to fly. Anything higher than the back of a horse gives you the creeps.'' Savannah stuck a dried pink rose in her hair, enhancing her already perfect appearance. ''I'm engaged, and I love Nathan with all my heart, but think of the exciting things Tanner has done.''

Charity watched her sister pout her perfectly full lips into a little bow that no male within a hundred miles could resist. That was the whole problem and had been since she'd turned thirteen. She sighed. ''Once I had dreams like that, but I've just stayed put here on the Ridge.''

Charity's eyes rolled to the top of her head. ''What about that year in New York?'' Where the sleazebag agent had tried to take advantage of her. ''And the six months in L.A.'' Where some jerk had promised her a film career for *favors*. Of course, there was also Billy Ray. Savannah's choice of men had left much to desire…until she'd woken up and discovered that the man of her dreams lived next door. *Hallelujah!*

Savannah gazed out the window. ''I was young then.''

''You're only twenty-nine now. Gray hair and Metamucil are a long way off,'' Charity quipped.

"Well, this is now, and Tanner Davenport's a true inspiration."

Charity's stomach tightened, her eyes crossed. She could barely breathe. Inspiration? Not another inspiration. Savannah's inspirations always came at the expense of good sense. Charity reached for a mint. "Tanner lives in an igloo and chews whale blubber. That's not inspiring. It's just cold."

"He doesn't live in an igloo, and I'm sure he never chewed blubber."

"You're going to have a great life with Nathan. You'll live in a big house and the only ice you'll have to think about will be in your mint julep on Derby day. Forget Alaska."

Savannah rolled her shoulders—shoulders men had lusted after along with her lips. "You have no imagination."

"I can't afford imagination."

"Of course you can, and I for one can't wait for Tanner to tell us his stories about Alaska. Think I'll have dinner at Thistledown tonight. Least I can do is spend an evening with my future husband and brother-in-law." Savannah tipped her perfect chin toward the kitchen. "I have a pot of chamomile brewing. Anyone care for a cup?" Savannah turned and sashayed back into the house.

Charity threw her hands in the air. She whispered to her mother, "Did you hear that? After a few Tanner-does-Alaska stories, Savannah will be on a road trip to heaven knows where. Then some loser guy will sweet-talk her out of her money, what's left of the farm, and end up breaking her heart again.''

''Least the share-of-the-farm thing only happened once.''

''Once was more than enough.'' Charity stood and paced. ''Savannah's marrying Nathan. Period. It's the best decision she's ever made. We all know it and she does, too. But what if she gets…sidetracked?''

Charity raked her hand through her hair. ''Why couldn't Tanner be an accountant instead of an Alaskan bush pilot? Then Savannah wouldn't want to hear any of his stories or care diddly what he'd been up to since she can't balance her own checkbook.''

Footsteps on the stones called her attention to the screen door and her approaching younger sister, Patience. At least, Charity thought it was Patience. Who else would be buried behind stems and leaves and roots dripping dirt everywhere other than the resident biologist home from college on spring break? Charity, Savannah, Patience. Oldest, middle, youngest. Horse farmer, beauty queen, plant nut. Sisters. Go figure.

Charity watched Patience pry open the door with the toe of her scuffed hiking boot and set the growth on the table. She wiped her hair from her cheek, leaving a brown smudge. She might be five-ten, willowy and gorgeously blond but, like Charity, Patience hadn't inherited the neat gene, either.

She beamed. ''Look what I found. *Prunus serotina*

growing in the lower pasture, or was it the upper? It was one of them. The dry spring brought them out in force. Thought I'd transplant some of the new starts by the front of the house."

Charity picked a leaf. "Looks like a black cherry tree with white stuff on the leaves."

"I just said it *was* a black cherry and that's larvae. It's spring, Charity. There are bugs."

"It's a fine tree. None better. Wonderful by the house, bugs and all." She looked at Patience. "But right now we have a bigger problem. You need to give me ideas on how to get Tanner Davenport interested in me."

Mama's jaw dropped. Patience's eyes bulged. Together they said, "Huh?"

Patience added, "Define 'interested.'"

"How about 'enthralled.'"

"Oh, brother. Why are you suddenly 'enthralled' with Tanner?" Eyeing Charity's dirty jeans and shirt, Patience gave her a suspicious look.

"I'm not. But it's our only hope to keep him from Savannah." Charity waggled her eyebrows at Patience. "Unless *you* want to do the honors."

"Not in a million. Why keep Tanner away from Savannah? They're friends. I didn't even know he was back on the Ridge."

"Well, he is. And I have to keep him busy for the next two weeks because if Savannah listens to his grand stories about Bigfoot or whatever else is up in

Alaska, she'll get a sudden attack of wanderlust and change her mind about marrying Nathan. You know she'd regret that decision for the rest of her life."

Charity spread her arms wide. A little melodrama never hurt. "It's a great idea. Right? We'll start with dinner tonight. Savannah's going to Thistledown, so we'll get Tanner over here." She beamed. "Tanner would go anywhere for Mama's fried chicken and corn bread."

Patience plucked a piece of hay from Charity's hair and straightened her collar. "Fried chicken and corn bread might tempt Tanner Davenport for dinner, but the enthralled part…" She let out a deep sigh. "If he was a horse, you'd have him, but Tanner's no horse. Have you considered kidnapping? We could just keep him in the barn for two weeks."

"Don't know about kidnapping, but I'll think of something."

Twenty minutes later Charity rode Ranger over the back path that, for as long as she could remember, had connected Thistledown to MacKay Farms. She stopped at the main house and was told Tanner was staying in one of the back cottages. She pulled Ranger up there, smoothed back her hair and straightened her clean blouse…now spotted with dust. If Puck hadn't taken the wagon into town, and if the pickup hadn't been on the fritz—again—and Savannah gone into work, Charity could have *driven* to Thistledown. Not that she minded riding, but once—just *once*—she needed to look nice. Nice enough to tempt Tanner.

She studied her rough hands and uneven fingernails. Okay, forget nice. The best she could hope for was presentable. And what chance did *presentable* have with Tanner Davenport, who undoubtedly had the entire female population of Alaska snapping at his heels? Slim to none, that's what. Being three years older than him didn't help, either. No fresh young thing here. Mama's chicken better have some darn good distracting powers.

Charity dismounted, tramped up the wooden steps and onto the porch, pulled in a deep breath, crossed her fingers and knocked. "Tanner? You in there, Tanner? Open up." No one answered, so she banged again. "Tanner?"

The door flew open and a sleepy-eyed, barechested, muscled Tanner stood in the entrance. "Charity?" His eyes widened. He rubbed them, then looked again. "What are you doing here?"

Salivating over you.

"Charity?"

A sprinkle of tan hair fell across his pecs and bisected his middle into two quadrants of fine, firm muscle. She swallowed. "Dinner."

"What about dinner?"

The soft curls disappeared below the waistband of the zipped but unbuttoned jeans that rode low on his narrow hips. "I have no idea."

"We'll talk later, when you make sense and I've had some sleep. I'm bushed."

He started to close the door, but she put her hands against it to stop him. She pulled her attention from his very fine torso to his face…rugged, unshaven, sleepy, sexy as all get-out. *Concentrate…and not on Tanner.* "I've come to ask you to dinner. Tonight. You said you loved Mama's fried chicken and she wants to welcome you into the family."

Charity eyed the front porch of the neat white clapboard cabin where she stood. Looking at him was not good for her equilibrium. Until this moment she hadn't known she had equilibrium. "Why aren't you staying in the main house?" She nodded at the big redbrick Georgian that his great-granddaddy had built more than a hundred years ago.

"It's better this way. Nate understands. You could have called, you know, and I'd really rather spend the night sleeping."

She pointed to the inside. "You can sleep back in Alaska. And the phone was busy," she lied.

Truth was, she didn't call at all because if Nathan had picked up, she hadn't wanted him to know about the invitation. He'd have told Savannah and then she would have wanted to stay home to talk to Tanner all night. Not to mention the fact that if Charity had called instead of dropping over, she would have missed this delicious encounter.

Tanner ran his hand over his face and shook his head as if trying to wake up.

"Mama's really counting on you coming." She was not above resorting to a little guilt-tripping to make this wedding happen. Once Nathan and her sister had tied the knot, there would be no more guys to treat Savannah like dirt. No more sleazebags to pay off with MacKay land. Nathan Davenport was a prince and would treat Savannah like a princess. And, he had enough land already.

Charity looked back at Tanner. His eyes were a bit more focused. They weren't as dark as before, more the shade of hot chocolate. Snuggling up with hot chocolate on a cold winter's night was wonderful; snuggling with Tanner would be even more wonderful. Of course, that would never happen, so why did she even think about such a thing? Tanner was a hunk, she was a…spinster? Well, not totally a spinster yet, but in a few years she'd have it nailed.

"Okay, I'll come. Wouldn't want to disappoint Mama Kay. And we'll have a chance to talk."

She spread her arms wide. "What do you call this?"

"About the wedding."

"Still no ideas on the gift, huh? We'll come up with something."

He gave her another of those long, steady looks. "Yeah, I really do have to come up with something.

Maybe I can convince you to help me. See you at seven.''

Charity mounted Ranger and turned in the direction of home. She looked back at Tanner who stood in the doorway—tall, magnificent, yummy. Common sense and good upbringing said, *Okay, Charity MacKay, it's time to turn around. Enough staring at the handsome man, this is really embarrassing.*

Ranger took the right bend in the lane and she turned a little farther left so as not to lose sight of Tanner…no shirt, no shoes, no idea what he did to her hormone level. She waved, he waved; then she turned a little more, lost her balance and slid clean out of the saddle, landing smack on her pride in the gravel. She hadn't fallen off a horse since…*ever.*

Tanner ran her way, concern on his face. She held up her hand to stop him as she got up, dusted herself off and called, "I'm fine. Terrific. Not hurt at all." *Except for my ego.* "See you tonight."

She forced a grin while thinking, *Ouch, ouch, ouch,* as her bones realigned. She remounted, missing the stirrup on the first try, and said to Ranger, "Don't you dare laugh, horse, or it's gruel for dinner." Whatever the heck gruel was.

She nudged Ranger into a trot and headed home. What was wrong with her? So Tanner Davenport was back. So he was a mouthwatering male. So he was the first male who had piqued her interest in thirty-two years, other than Tommy Jones. She and Tommy were pretty good together; for a while she had thought he might be *the one*. Then Golden Rod had come down with colic, and there'd been no time for Tommy. He hadn't understood that horses came first.

But this was now, and Tanner was not Tommy, but he was still all wrong for her. That's the part she had to remember. A struggling horse farmer in Kentucky with latent acrophobia and enough responsibilities to last two lifetimes was no match for an adventurous, handsome flyboy from Alaska.

All she had to do was to keep Tanner away from Savannah until she married Nathan. After that Tanner could take his great body, dynamite smile and intriguing brown eyes and fly back to his iceberg. Then everything would return to normal.

Chapter Two

The late-afternoon sun inched toward the horizon as Tanner approached the white brick MacKay farmhouse, which was surrounded by pink azaleas and purple rhododendron. Green sprigs of weeping willow drifted on a breeze and the old magnolia by the kitchen sported white blossoms bigger than his hand.

As he headed for the barns, the aroma of Southern-fried chicken wafting through the back door made his mouth water in anticipation. Saturday-night dinner at the MacKay farm, how great was that? Then he thought of Charity and her creamy skin and sparkling eyes and knew it was damn terrific.

She intrigued him, but he didn't need intriguing. He needed to talk to her about the wedding and to not get involved with her in any other way because he wasn't staying. Alaska was his home now—the place that made him happy when Kentucky never could. He pushed Charity from his mind and concentrated on the aroma of fried chicken. That's what he'd do from here on, replace thoughts of Charity with food. He spotted Puck and Charity by the stables as she scowled and kicked a rock across the driveway. "Blast that man!"

"For once I'm innocent," Tanner countered. "I just got here." He nodded a greeting at Puck, who was tall, lean, forever wise and the best horse trainer in the state. Not to mention the best friend the MacKays had ever had. Hell, he was the best friend Tanner had ever had…besides Nate.

Puck chuckled. "You're off the hook this time, Alaska. It's Billy Ray who's got Charity's dander up. She just came back from a less-than-pleasant meeting with the man."

Charity's eyes smoldered. "I'm going to strangle my ex-brother-in-law with my bare hands." She looked at Tanner. "And you're early."

Her hair hung in tangles, as if she'd ridden like the wind from wherever she'd been. Her cheeks were flushed, her eyes stormy. This went beyond intriguing and straight to sexy as hell.

No, no. He couldn't think about Charity as sexy. He'd get himself into another embarrassing condition impossible to explain. *Think food.* Crispy-fried chicken, tons of gravy. "I'm early because *somebody* woke me out of a sound sleep and I couldn't go back. And I wanted to see if you were all right since your fall off Ranger. What's your beef with Billy Ray?"

Puck's gray eyes widened. He gaped at Charity,

then stuffed his hands into his pockets and rocked back on his heels. "*You* fell off a horse?"

"Billy Ray's my ex-brother-in-law, as of two and a half years ago. He and Savannah were married for six months, the longest six months in the history of mankind."

Tanner shook his head. "Billy Ray's a jerk, always wanting something for nothing. Can't count the number of times he tried to con me out of my biplane. Why would Savannah marry him?"

"I imagine the marriage proposal went something like, 'Come with me, baby, and see the U.S.A. on the back of my Harley.' She was young and naive and went with him, but the only thing she saw was his miserable excuse of a farm and a lot of grief. At the time we didn't have two dimes to rub together, so I gave him fifty acres of prime MacKay land in the divorce settlement just to get him away from her. I'm trying to buy it back. Rumor has it he's selling it off…to somebody else. Won't even consider my offer. Blast that man!"

Puck scowled. "He treated Savannah pitiful. One of these days somebody's going to take him apart. Hope I'm around to see it." He looked to Charity. "You really fell off Ranger?"

She gave him a slit-eyed look. "Bet Mama needs help in the kitchen. There's rice pudding for dessert. Bet you could sneak some."

Puck turned for the house, saying, "Rice pudding

might save you now, but not forever, Charity MacKay.''

''I know, I know. For the next thirty years I'll be hearing about falling off—''

''Ha, you're not getting off that easy.''

Charity smiled but a worry line still creased her forehead, and Tanner was sure it had nothing to do with falling off Ranger. It was the fifty acres. Losing part of her farm must have been like losing part of herself.

He wanted to hold her, to sooth the worry away. But he didn't know how to erase the burden of years of so many responsibilities. He tucked a strand of hair behind her ear, letting his hand linger against her cheek for a moment because he felt the overwhelming need to do something for her, no matter how insignificant.

She looked at him, her emerald eyes filled with surprise, her lips parted just a breath. Oh, how he wanted to kiss those soft, sweet lips. He wanted it bad. But that sure as hell wouldn't keep his mind off her. Her body seemed to be leaning toward his, her eyes luring him closer. Just one little kiss? *Bad idea.* ''When…when do we eat?''

''Eat?'' Her eyes flew wide open and she took a step back as if she, too, had suddenly realized what they'd been about to do was a really bad idea. ''Ah…soon.'' We should do something in the meantime…like check on the horses. Come with me and meet Misty Kay. The pride and joy of MacKay Farms.''

He fell into step beside Charity, keeping his mind on dinner and not on her fine shape or the way she held her head just so. They rounded the old wooden water trough and headed for the second stable. She seemed shorter, more fragile. His chest tightened a fraction. Charity MacKay was a lot of things, but he never remembered her being fragile...till now. "Tell me about Billy Ray."

"That horse's ass has our land, end of story. You planning on wearing that bomber jacket the whole time you're here? Gotta tell you, not much to bomb on the Ridge, flyboy."

He grinned. "Now *that's* the Charity I remember."

She stopped and gazed up at him, her eyes softening to moss-green. Dang.

"What do you mean?"

He meant that she had the most incredible eyes he'd ever seen, the kind that told her every mood, her every thought. The kind he could get lost in—but wouldn't. Alaska was his home, not here. *Black sheep didn't graze on family land*—least that's the way his daddy had put it when he'd kicked him out. "You seem more yourself now."

"I'm just me. Don't have time to be anything else."

And he believed that. He parked his left foot on the rim of the trough and looked around. The barn door needed a new hinge and one of the buckets by the trough had a hole in its side. Anyone who thought houses were money pits had never lived on a horse farm.

"When I left here, your stepdaddy had gambled the farm into the ground. You must have worked your hind end off to get the place where it is now."

Charity gave him a sly grin. "Yeah, but the old goat took off when the money ran out, and my hind end's still intact." She patted her backside and Tanner's eyes followed. Nice, very nice. Heat crept into her cheeks, then his. They looked at each other. What was she thinking? What the heck was *he* thinking? Where was that chicken when he needed it?

Charity cut her eyes to the stable. "You really ought to meet Misty."

She snagged the sleeve of his jacket and yanked him toward the stable, nearly toppling him into the trough. Not that it would be all bad. He could do with a little dunking in cold water.

"Puck probably helped you keep the farm together," he said, attempting to keep his mind off the auburn streaks in her hair. "I know Patience didn't do much or there'd be trees in the stalls instead of horses, and Savannah would have *Ralph Lauren* and *Gucci* stenciled on the roofs."

See, he could keep his mind off Charity. He relaxed a little, feeling more in control. Everything seemed normal.

"Actually, your dad helped a lot."

"*My* dad?" He stopped walking. What was that about normal? His dad helping was not normal. His dad bellowing at him to take more of an interest in the farm and to do things his way was normal.

"He gave me a job, I paid attention. He must have answered a million questions. In fact, he lent me the money to buy a horse from Billy Ray that he couldn't do anything with. Puck turned Gray Goblin around and we won a few races. I think that's why Billy Ray went after Savannah. I took his horse and made him a winner. He took my sister and then my land. Wonderful man. We sure do miss him and stepdad at the family get-togethers."

"My dad was a big help?"

"Beyond big. I know you two didn't always get along."

Understatement of the century. Tanner couldn't remember them seeing eye-to-eye on anything—except Nathan. Dad had thought Nathan the perfect son. Tanner agreed: he was the perfect brother. Too bad he was always caught in the middle of a family feud that could never be settled. "You could probably hear Dad and me yelling all the way to your house."

"You have his eyes, you know. And the cleft in your chin. How do you shave in there?"

"Teeny-tiny razors." He shook his head again. "My dad?"

She yanked his sleeve again and tugged him on.

They entered the barn and Charity nodded at a horse, with a beautiful black coat and soft brown eyes, peeking out of a stall. "She's due to foal next week."

Tanner shook his head, trying to straighten out his thoughts. His dad helped Charity. Tanner couldn't remember his dad ever helping anyone. He had the temperament of a bulldozer. "She's gorgeous."

"She's the price Billy Ray set for the land."

For the second time in less than five minutes Tanner felt as if he'd been slapped upside the head. "He wants your horse for the fifty acres?"

"And foal." She kissed the mare. "I wouldn't give that no good, low-down varmint so much as a stray cat. Billy Ray's not mistreating another living thing as long as I'm alive to stop him."

She reached into her pocket and offered Misty a sugar cube. "You're going to be a good mama, aren't you, girl? The best ever, and in three years that healthy baby you're carrying will make the Run for The Roses and race the MacKay green-and-blue silks straight into the Derby winner's circle where they were twenty years ago."

The determination in Charity's voice impressed him, more than anything had impressed him in a long time. She'd worked her whole life for this, and he knew all about working for what was important and the sacrifices it took to make it happen. "That's a mighty tall order for one little foal."

"It's a beginning. Finally." She nodded at the

other stalls. "I have three more mares ready to foal. Two go to auction. I'll get the creditors off our backs once and for all and repay the loans."

Tanner stroked the mare. "Paying for the wedding has to be a strain."

"Savannah's paying for her dress, Nathan's doing the reception, and we can manage the rest."

He gave her a long, steady look, then said, "Maybe there shouldn't be a wedding."

"Huh?" Her brow furrowed right on top of the furrow that was already there.

Dang, now he was adding to her problems and that's not what he wanted to do at all. In fact, he wanted to avoid problems; he had to make her see that. "Look, Charity, I know you have a lot on your mind, but this wedding between Nate and Savannah is crazy."

"What are you talking about? The wedding's going to be perfect."

"Yeah, but what about after the wedding? What about the marriage?" He ran his hand around his neck. "Savannah's a...a wild child."

"*You* calling someone else wild? That's the pot calling the kettle black. Besides, Savannah is *not* a wild child." Charity tipped her chin and assumed a superior stance. "She's a little spirited at times, that's all."

"A bottle of Kentucky bourbon is spirited. Savannah's high-test moonshine."

Charity's back went straight as a fence post. "Well, she's darn good moonshine."

"Amen to that. Just not for Nate."

"I don't get it. You and Savannah were always friends, were in the same grade, hung with the same crowd, got grounded for the same shenanigans. Thought you'd be a little more supportive."

"Nate is Bill Gates's clone and Savannah's the life of the party. Hell, she's the life of the whole damn town. Sure gives everyone something to talk about, especially since I'm not here. Did she tell you about the time—"

"I don't want to know."

"Exactly my point."

"So this is why you wanted to talk to me about the wedding, to break it up? What does Nathan think of your great idea?"

"He's not listening."

"No wonder you're sleeping in the outhouse."

"It's a cabin and I'm sleeping there because I want to. Every time I go in the front door I can still hear my dad…" Tanner let out a big breath he didn't realize he'd been holding in. "But that's not important. What matters now is that Nathan and Savannah don't see that the marriage is headed for disaster. Savannah's never stuck with anything in her life. She'll tire of Nate and leave him and break his heart."

"So…so what do you intend to do? Got any great

plans? Lock Nathan away in the attic? Marry Savannah off to a band of Gypsies?''

''Nothing that manipulative. All I'm going to do is remind Nate and Savannah of the obvious, that they're complete opposites and want different things in life. They'll break up on their own. Savannah doesn't want to be stuck on the Ridge. She doesn't want to spend the next sixty years here any more than I do. I'll remind her there's a big wonderful world out there waiting to be discovered. She's reaching for Nate because he's convenient. Nate likes the simple life, and there is not one thing simple about Savannah. He's just spellbound.''

Charity felt her head spin and her hands sweat. Not only did she have to deal with Savannah being *inspired,* now there was Mr. Know-it-all from the frozen tundra trying to break up the marriage. *What was she going to do?*

Insisting the marriage would happen was like waving smoked salmon in front of an Alaskan grizzly. She needed a tranquilizing dart for Tanner like the kind used on ''Wild Kingdom'' where they shoot the bear in the butt and put him to sleep before he knows what has hit him—though Tanner's butt was a lot nicer than a grizzly's. Just the same, she needed to put Tanner to sleep, butt and all—or at least to throw him off guard. She eyed him. *Ready, aim…* ''Maybe you're right.''

''I am.'' His eyes rounded.

She pulled in a deep, soul-searching breath and wrung her hands in fake concern. She paced to the side and back again as if lost in thought. She would have to give an Oscar-caliber performance to convince Tanner she was sincere. She stopped pacing and looked at him. "Yeah, you really are."

"Hmm."

"Now that I think about it and hear your side of the story, I realize the wedding is doomed, just as you said. Talking to you makes things clear as well water."

He didn't seem convinced. She thumped her forehead with the palm of her hand and paced. "How could I have been so blind? I got so caught up in wedding dresses and being maid of honor and shades of green and peach blossom and orchids and three hundred guests at Thistledown that I lost sight of the big picture, of whether Nathan and Savannah make a good match. I was mesmerized with the wedding plans."

She put her hands to her face in consternation, then peeked through a slit in her fingers. Did he buy it?

"You're trying out for an Oscar, right?"

How did he know? This was not the same guy who left the Ridge years ago. He was mature and worldly wise—two qualities she didn't need at the moment. She needed a lackluster pushover who would think this marriage was the best thing since sliced bread and would go along with her every wish. *Fat chance that*. She'd have to come up with something else, something big, to make him believe her.

She dropped her hands. "I suppose I wanted this marriage so much I didn't face the truth when it was right in front of me." She nodded with each word. "And to show you I mean what I say, I'll…I'll help you break it off."

"You will." It was a disbelieving statement and not a question. She had to convince him.

"Definitely. 'Course we have to be discreet. Discretion is very important." Mostly because she didn't want Nathan and Savannah to know what was going on so this happy time wouldn't be ruined for them. "If Nathan and Savannah think we're trying to split them up, they'll just dig in their heels more, and maybe even elope. *Merciful heaven*." She let out a forbidding sigh and put the back of her hand to her forehead in a swoon pose.

He gave her a questioning look, as if she was one fry short of a Happy Meal. Maybe she was overdoing it a bit. She flashed him an agreeable smile. "What I mean is, we'll have to formulate a plan." *And I'll formulate one that will make sure this wedding goes off without a hitch.* "And we'll have to hurry." *I'll hurry and think of a way to stop you.* "With the two of us working on this, how can the marriage happen at all?" *But it will, if it takes my last breath. Savannah's going to live happily ever after and the rest of*

MacKay Farms will be safe from no-good husbands.
"It's a great idea."

"What's cooking in that brain of yours, Kentucky Girl?"

"Me?" Did she sound innocent? She really hoped so.

"Whatever it is, it won't keep *me* from stopping this wedding."

She assumed a wounded look and spread her arms wide. "Didn't you hear a word I said, Tanner Davenport? I'm helping you. You convinced me. I'm with you all the way. You win."

"Then why don't I feel like I've won?"

He ran his hand through his rich brown hair. She wanted to do that. Then run her hands over his broad chest, tight midsection, narrow waist and below to… to…*holy cow.*

"And if what you're saying is true, it's the first time you've listened to anyone in your life."

She focused on Tanner's words instead of his nicely put-together body. It wasn't nearly as much fun. "Look, I'm trying to be helpful. I think you should take me up on my offer. Both of us working on the same side has got to be a good thing."

His eyes narrowed. "If you're double-crossing me, Charity…"

Mama called, announcing dinner. Charity took Tanner's hand to reassure him of her sincerity and good intentions. To distract him from the sign she imagined was on her forehead flashing I Am Guilty As Sin. But suddenly the wedding and her deception weren't that important; the only thing on her mind was Tanner's hand—warm, strong, capable, dependable—in hers. It felt good. Great, in fact. She didn't want to let it go.

An old scar jagged across the knuckle of his third finger and his palm felt rough. He worked hard. She looked up at him. He was so darn handsome, so much a…man, and so much a total pain.

She had to concentrate on the last attribute and to ignore his very manly attributes. She and Tanner had nothing in common, and they stood on opposite sides of the Savannah/Nathan wedding fence. This was not the stuff relationships, even very short relationships, were made of. Reluctantly she let go of his hand. "We'd better go inside. Mama will send the hounds after us."

"You don't have hounds."

"Trust me, she'll find some." They made their way to the house, side by side, as they'd done many times in the past. But this wasn't the past. Now Tanner Davenport was a *babe*.

Criminy! Life could be as frustrating as a woodpecker drumming on a tin chimney, especially when it threw Tanner in her path and said *Hands off!*

CHARITY COULDN'T BELIEVE it was already Monday morning. She sipped her coffee and looked out the kitchen window. What the heck happened to Sunday? Oh, yeah, she'd repaired a fence damaged by overhanging tree limbs in the south pasture. She scratched a bug bite on her wrist. A lot of insects this time of year and they all wanted her for lunch.

At least Tanner hadn't been around to worry her into an early grave. He'd slept the whole day, bless his little heart. She hadn't worried about how Tanner intended to break up the engagement or whether Savannah was hanging on his every word about life on a glacier and catching a terminal case of wanderlust.

Now there were only twelve days left to worry about. 'Course that meant Charity had twelve more days to resist looking into Tanner's deep brown eyes and salivating over his hunky body. But she could do it. He wasn't all that irresistible and twelve days wasn't *that* long.

She turned as Puck came into the kitchen followed by Mama, who said, "There's yogurt in the fridge, dear. I made tuna salad for lunch. I'm going into town for a garden club luncheon."

Thank heaven for the garden club. It was one of the few clubs in town that hadn't snubbed Mama when the MacKay money ran out. Charity's jaw clenched as she poured coffee. How could anyone snub Mama?

Puck sat at the kitchen table. "Station wagon's been acting up." He glanced at Mama. "I should drive you into town. Don't want you stranded on the four-lane."

Mama smiled at him. "Well, that's mighty considerate of you."

Charity glanced from them to the window to the rusted heap parked next to the house. "We need to replace that thing. It's not safe. Maybe…maybe this fall."

"No need to go doing that," Puck replied. "The wagon and I understand each other, and I don't mind driving Margaret now and then. Don't mind at all." He cleared his throat and continued. "One of Nathan's mares is off her feed and I said I'd stop by Thistledown on the way back and take a look-see."

He glanced at his watch and stood. "Think I'll check on Silver Bell. She doesn't seem quite right this morning, either. I'll be ready at noon."

Charity sipped her coffee and heard the screen door slam shut behind Puck. It was so nice that Mama and Puck were friends. Had been for years, through the bad times and now the good. "Where were you and Puck so early this morning?"

Mama's cheeks pinked. Springtime made everyone look healthy, especially Mama. She said, "We…went down to the orchard and cut back some of the dead wood on the trees. We should have a good crop of apples this year."

"You don't have to cut trees, Mama. I can help Puck do those things."

"I enjoyed it."

"Puck is good company."

"Yes. Yes, he is." Mama fiddled with her coffee cup. "Besides you've got enough on your mind with the wedding and all. Is Tanner excited about the engagement? He didn't say much at dinner the other night."

Charity stood and refilled her cup. She leaned against the yellow Formica counter. "We have a little problem. Tanner's not keen on the wedding."

Mama smiled. "He'll come around. He's very protective of Nathan even though Nathan's the oldest. Everybody knows Nathan used to stand up for Tanner against his daddy and even tried to patch things over once Tanner left. But with two hardheads it takes a powerful lot of patching."

"Tanner wants to break up the engagement."

Mama sipped her coffee and shook her head. "I'm not all that surprised. From where Tanner stands this doesn't look like a match made in heaven."

"I told him I'd help."

Mama dropped her cup, spilling coffee everywhere. Charity grabbed a towel. "Don't panic, I'm not really going to help him, just pretend. That way I'll have an excuse to be around and get to know his plans. I can head him off before he messes things up. Brilliant, huh?"

Mama shook her head as she took the towel to the sink. "I think you're in way over your head, dear. If

Tanner finds out that you're flimflamming him, he'll be madder than—''

''He won't find out. How could he? You and I are the only ones who know.''

''Know what?'' Tanner's voice came from the doorway into the hall.

Charity froze. *Uh-oh!* She plastered a smile on her face and turned to Tanner. Why hadn't she heard him drive up? The path! Darn.

''I saw Puck out front and he told me to come in,'' Tanner explained. He turned from Mama to Charity. ''Hope I'm not interrupting anything.''

''No, no,'' Charity said in too much of a rush. ''I mean, we, Mama and I, were just talking girl talk. It's early. Why are you here? Don't you need more sleep?''

Mama gave her a scolding look. ''Don't be rude, dear. I'm sure Tanner would like some coffee and I just opened a fresh jar of grape marmalade.''

Tanner pulled a chair up to the table and sat. ''Thanks. That sounds delicious.'' He glanced at Charity. ''Food is always good, especially around here. Is Savannah awake?''

''Why?'' Charity blurted out.

''Charity!'' Mama looked at Tanner and wagged her head. ''I have no idea who raised this girl.'' She handed Charity the marmalade. ''Now if you'll both excuse me, I have a luncheon to attend.''

Tanner seemed even more handsome today…was

that possible? Clean-shaven, no roadmap eyes and he'd shed his jacket. It wasn't glued to his skin, after all. But then she knew that because she'd seen his skin up close and personal. Fine muscles, a sprinkle of hair, broad shoulders and six-pack abs. Hormonal meltdown threatened.

"I have a plan."

"To break up the engagement, no doubt."

His expression turned hard. "You don't sound happy about the idea."

"Hey, I'm happy." She flashed a grin she hoped didn't look as phony as it felt. "Thrilled."

"I'll take Savannah flying. She loves to fly. It'll remind her that she wants to see the world. Great idea, isn't it?"

Yeah, blooming stupendous. "Don't you miss Alaska? Think of it. Bears, eagles, frostbite? What about your business? Who's flying all those bushes when you're not around?"

"I have a partner. He's flying bushes just fine without me—thank you for being so concerned—and I will go back as soon as I convince Savannah that the last thing she wants is to be married to my brother. You're not acting very supportive. Having second thoughts on breaking up the engagement?"

"No, of course not. I'm just not sure flying's the answer. Besides, Savannah's at work. She's a receptionist at Doc Waverley's and gets off at five. You can see her later." *About twelve days later, after she's married to Nathan.*

"Maybe I'll go into town and see her at Doc's."

"You can't." Charity took a deep breath and tried not to panic. "What I mean is, Mondays are really busy at the office and…and you have other things to do today."

"I don't even live here. What could I possibly have to do?"

This was getting very complicated. What could she come up with to keep him away from Savannah? Something. *Anything.* "You have…the talks…at the school. On Alaska. And the talk this evening at the library." Not too bad considering the short notice.

"Me?"

"Know anyone else around here who lives in Alaska?" He didn't have to do those talks *yet,* but he would as soon as she made some calls to the school and the library. They'd be thrilled to have someone give a first-hand account of what it was like to live in Alaska. "Didn't anyone from the school or library get hold of you?"

Suspicion lit his eyes. "Tell me, Kentucky Girl, how do *you* know all this when I don't?"

She tipped her head, assuming an air of confidence while racking her brain for an answer and hoping she didn't get struck dead for telling so many lies. "At the Pick and Pack, of course. Ground Zero for gossip. When I went for groceries. Yesterday. Guess you missed the messages. But you'll have to do the talks, can't disappoint all those people and the kids. Can't disappoint the kids. Good thing I brought it up, huh?''

He studied her for a moment and she did the same to him. Would she ever tire of looking at him? Dark eyes, firm lips, determined chin.

''Breakfast,'' he said, bringing her back to the moment. ''You wouldn't happen to have any extra, would you? Ham? Eggs? Biscuits? An omelet or two lying around? I *really* miss Kentucky food.'' He studied her for another moment. ''I need to think about food more while I'm here. It's a great distraction.''

''Distraction from what?''

He sighed and looked out the window. ''Stuff. All kinds of stuff.'' He turned back to her. ''You'd be amazed at what stuff. I sure as hell am.''

''I think you've flipped your lid.'' She nodded at the fridge. ''There's all kinds of food in there. Help yourself. I should go into town with you. To the library and the schools.''

''No, no.'' He held up his hands as if warding off a herd of wild horses that threatened to trample him. ''You don't have to do that. I'm fine. *You* stay here. I'll go alone. I know my way around.''

''Now what kind of neighbor would I be if I abandoned you? I'll introduce you to the new principal and the librarian.''

''Maybe I'll run into Savannah?''

Not if I have to break both your legs. ''You know,

you and your father have a lot in common, like a one-tracked mind.''

His jaw suddenly clenched. ''I'm nothing like my father.''

She rolled her eyes so far back in her head she saw where her ears attached. ''Yeah, right. Look, I need to make a few phone calls. Business. I'll shower and change and come back in a few minutes. We'll get a car at Thistledown and be on our way.''

''A few minutes?''

''You'd be surprised what I can do when motivated.'' She sighed out a breath. ''And lately I've been motivated like crazy.''

She darted from the kitchen and headed for the main hall and the stairs, calling over her shoulder, ''Don't move a muscle.'' *And heaven knows he had more than his share to move.*

She stopped on the fifth step and looked back toward the kitchen. Muscles? Why did she keep thinking about Tanner's muscles…and his incredible eyes and lips and how handsome he was?

She plunked her head against the wall. Was there a twelve-step program for idiots? This obsession with Tanner Davenport made no sense at all. He was three years younger, Savannah's friend, and they had nothing in common, proven by the fact that he'd left a horse farm she'd give her eyeteeth for and had gone to Alaska to fly airplanes. *Who would do such a thing?*

But he *was* a hunk. No twelve-step or one-hundred-and-twelve-step program could change that.

Chapter Three

Tanner followed Charity out the main doors of Blue-grass Ridge Elementary, then down the steps. ''That was great. I had a terrific time.''

For the millionth time he glanced at Charity. Gray skirt, bulky white sweater that hinted at soft curves beneath, long shapely legs and red hair that swayed as she walked.

He swallowed a groan. All morning while he and Charity went from one classroom to another he'd tried to keep his eyes off her and to concentrate on Alaska. But now he had nothing to focus on but... ''We need food.''

They walked down the street toward the heart of town as she asked, ''Is that story about a moose chasing you true or did you make it up?''

She smiled at him and for a second he forgot where he was. She could do that to him. Make him forget everything but her. ''If that guy could have climbed trees, I'd be an ornament on his antlers right now.

One of the joys of living in Moose Crossing. Moose are mean critters, and they have terrible breath.''

"The scary thing is that you know *firsthand* they have terrible breath."

They shared a laugh and Tanner wanted nothing more than to put his arm around her and to bring her close as they walked along. It felt as if it would be the natural thing to do. But it wasn't. It would be a dumb thing to do because it would suggest there was something between them when there never could be. "Let's have a big lunch."

"Do you think of anything besides eating?"

He watched sunshine play in her hair. "Unfortunately, yes."

They crossed Center Street and headed for the Sizzling Skillet. "Look." He pointed up the street. "Isn't that Savannah coming out of Elegant Essentials? Bet she has time for lunch, after all."

He snatched Charity's hand. "This is great. I can ask her about flying. Maybe she can make it tomorrow after work."

"But…but…"

He tugged her toward the boutique, calling for Savannah to wait up.

She beamed when she spied him. "What are you doing here, Tanner Davenport? And with my big sister. How did you ever get her out of the barns?"

"It was her idea."

Savannah's eyes brightened and her mouth gaped.

"Well, if that don't beat all. The age of miracles is not dead."

Tanner hooked his other arm through Savannah's. "Now I'm taking you two to lunch."

Savannah shook her head. "Forget food. I've got a better idea."

Tanner glanced at Charity. "There isn't a better idea than food. Least, that's what I keep telling myself."

Savannah guided him and Charity toward the boutique. "I need a man's advice on perfume. I want something new, something daring, something passionate and exciting for my wedding." She giggled. "Make that *wedding night.*" She let go of Tanner and spread her hands wide. "Help me, you guys?"

"You can do that later, you don't need us," Tanner replied. "Besides, I want to talk to you about going fly—"

"If Savannah wants our help," Charity said, ushering Tanner up the steps of the boutique, "we'll help her. What kind of perfume did you have in mind?" she asked Savannah, then whispered to Tanner, "Part of being discreet. We have to be discreet or Savannah will suspect we're up to something and get suspicious."

He whispered in return, "What about the flying idea? I was just going to tell her about that. And what does perfume have to do with discretion?"

"You'd be surprised."

The shop was full of lace and silk flowers, with lotions and perfumes and bath things on counters. Oh, yeah, he fit in here all right. He greeted the salesladies then leaned against the doorjamb, close to the exit, taking it all in. Well, if nothing else, this was a new experience.

Savannah picked up a jade-green glass bottle and removed the stopper. She put a dot on the inside of her wrist and held it up to Tanner.

His eyes watered. "A little heavy."

Savannah wiggled her brows. "It's called *Bondage*."

Tanner's mouth dropped wide open and he righted himself from the jamb. "For Nathan?"

Savannah sprayed her other wrist and smiled wickedly. "This one's Orgy."

Tanner coughed. "Don't they have something like Profit And Loss or Winner's Circle? That's more Nathan."

Savannah giggled again. "You have no imagination, Tanner Davenport. And you don't know your brother half as well as you think you do."

She snatched Charity's arm. "I'm all out of wrists. We'll use yours."

Charity took a little strip of white paper from the counter. "Just dab some on this. I don't think I'm up to Bondage or Orgy."

Savannah tisked and waved her hands. "Charity, Charity, Charity. You may know gobs and gobs about horses, but you know nothing about perfume. It must have the heat of your skin to react.''

Savannah picked up a ruby-colored bottle, took out the stopper and dabbed Charity. She dragged Charity's wrist to Tanner and brought it to his face. "What about this? It's called Ravish. What do you think?''

Charity and Ravish together right in front of him? How'd he get roped into this? He swallowed, his eyes fogged. Did the room just move? Where was lunch when he needed it? *Ravish!*

Savannah explained, "Perfume reacts differently depending on where it's placed on the body. A drop behind the knee gives off a different fragrance than one between a woman's breasts. Did you know that, Tanner?''

Charity didn't move, but Savannah took her other wrist and offered it to Tanner. "This one's called Vamp.''

The heat from Charity's body seeped into his. His mouth went as dry as a pond in summer. Charity took a step back and, plopping down onto a purple-cushioned stool, put her head between her knees. "I think I'm allergic.''

"I know I am.'' Tanner ran his hand through his hair and swallowed. "Food. I need to think about food.''

Charity glanced his way as she sipped the water one of the salesladies brought to her. "Why don't you weigh five-hundred pounds?''

"We should go. *I* should go."

Savannah put her hands to her hips. "But which perfume? That was the whole point of us coming here. Remember?"

"Not Ravish or Vamp," Charity and Tanner said at the same time. Tanner's gaze collided with hers. For a second, breathing seemed impossible.

Savannah looked from Charity to Tanner and back. She wagged her head, a slow grin on her lips. "Well, I'll be a monkey's uncle." There was a twinkle in her eye. "Who would have thought that you two were mutually…allergic."

Tanner said, "You'd be a monkey's *aunt* and I'll wait outside because I can't think at *all* in here."

He hobbled down the steps of the boutique in hormone-induced agony and stood behind a bench on the sidewalk to hide his condition. He'd been hiding his condition one hell of a lot lately. Savannah came out first and asked him, "Want to know which fragrance I chose? Bondage." She grinned like a teenager and sashayed like a stripper.

Charity came up behind her and laughed. "I have the feeling Nathan Davenport is in for one heck of a wedding night."

Savannah looked at her sister. "Wait till we go lingerie shopping. But right now I must get back to work, and you two should spend some time together."

"Why would you say that?" Charity asked.

"For an older sister, you sure don't have all the answers." She laughed, patted Tanner's cheek as if he were a little boy, and turned for her office.

"What's with Savannah?" Charity wondered.

"Beats me." Whiffs of Ravish and Vamp floated his way. "But I think we should eat *now.*"

CHARITY CLOSED the front door behind her as the hall clock bonged out 9:00 p.m. and Mama Kay came around the corner, cradling a cup in her hands. "Would you like some cinnamon tea, dear? I find it so comforting this time of night when…"

She eyed Charity's clothes and stopped dead. "Where have you been?" Her eyes shot wide open. "Oh, merciful heaven. Did I miss a funeral? Mrs. Wakefield? I knew she was poorly. Can't believe someone at the garden club didn't mention—"

"It wasn't a funeral, Mama. I was out with Tanner." Never in all her born days did she think she'd utter *those* words.

Her mother's eyes widened more. "Tanner? You and Tanner?"

"Not *out* like that. Out like keeping him away from Savannah so he doesn't interfere with the wedding."

She hopped on one foot, pulling off a shoe, then did the same on the other foot while bouncing her way toward the stairs. "I now know more about the great state of Alaska than anyone in Kentucky ever wanted to."

"Did you have a good time?"

Charity stopped mid-hop. "Tanner's rescued tourists from glaciers, mountaintops and boats. There are no roads into the capital city and that means he flies a lot of people there in all kinds of weather. You can actually see whales from the western shores, and he says the aurora borealis is incredible."

She started up the stairs as Mama replied, "That is interesting, dear. Very interesting, indeed."

"Mama, do not read anything into this. Tanner is handsome, I'll give you that. And I realize you and Savannah and Puck have always liked him. But *trouble* was his middle name since the day he was born and now he's a poster boy for Adventures-R-Me. I have enough adventure taking care of this place and I do not need *trouble*. I've had my quota. If there are two people on earth with less in common than Charity MacKay and Mr. Alaska, I can't guess who they'd be. The reason I was with him involved…business, strictly business."

Mama tipped her chin. "You sure do have an awful lot to say about a man you don't care two hoots about."

Charity spread her arms wide, a shoe dangling from each hand. "I'm trying to make myself clear, that's all. Now I've got to get out of these clothes and into some jeans and check on the horses."

Charity continued up the stairs as Mama said, "Puck and I checked the horses earlier. They seem fine enough, though Silver Bell hadn't eaten much. Probably from the change in season. It'll do that to a horse now and then. In the morning, try adding a dash of ground malt to coax her along.''

Charity stopped, then retraced her path down the stairs. She leaned against the old mahogany newel worn smooth from so many hands and behinds sliding over the top. She studied her mother. "*You* went to the barns and checked the horses? You haven't been out there in…I don't know how long.''

"Puck asked me to." A smile touched her soft lips and her blue eyes twinkled. "Don't look so surprised. At one time I nearly lived in those stables, same as you do now. It was my granddaddy who built this farm, if you remember." She sighed, but her eyes stayed bright. Something Charity hadn't seen in a very long while.

"Actually, I didn't remember much myself until Puck and I started talking about it in the car today on the way to Thistledown,'' Mama added. "Made me remember what it was like around here before… before…''

"Forget *before,* Mama. We all have.''

Mama's eyes misted. "But you and your sisters didn't have an easy time of it growing up, all because I married the wrong man. After your father died I felt so confused. I know horses but not the horse business. I thought marriage would take care of that.'' She gave Charity a wary smile. "Big mistake.''

Charity came to her mother and kissed her cheek. "In the beginning he wasn't so bad. Just later on when he realized it was more fun to bet on horses than to care for them. Hey, a lot of people have it a lot worse. We always had each other and the farm. Think of now. Think of the good times ahead. The wedding. Patience graduating from college. The new foals due anytime. No regrets."

Charity nodded toward the door. "I'll be in the stables. If you want to come visit, that would be wonderful."

She watched her mother head for the front porch, then Charity climbed the stairs. She hadn't seen Mama like this in a long, long time. Hopeful. She stood in the middle of her room and took a deep breath, closed her eyes and savored the moment.

Right now, this very instant, everything seemed perfect. It didn't happen often, not often at all, but holding on to the perfect times is what got her through the tough ones. *That* she knew from experience.

THE NEXT MORNING Charity stood at the back window sipping orange juice and watching spring come to Kentucky. The hills, turning blue with new grass, were dotted with patches of yellow buttercups, bluebells, purple cress, red buds and pink lady's slippers. Her whole being seemed to come alive just taking it all in. She couldn't imagine living anywhere else. But somewhere deep inside she wanted to have someone to share it with. Someone to care about, and who cared about her. Deeply, intimately.

But that didn't look as if it would happen. And... and that was okay. No pity parties. Heck, after what she'd been through to save the farm she'd be downright delirious with happiness for the rest of her days just taking care of the horses and watching the farm prosper. Right?

She pulled in a deep breath. Of course, right! Everything was great.

Just look how things were going with Savannah and Tanner. That situation couldn't be better. She'd kept Savannah away from Tanner so she wouldn't be inspired by his tales of Alaska, and she'd kept Tanner from asking Savannah to go flying and reminding her what she was missing by marrying Nathan.

Today brought round two. Savannah had to work, so that would keep her from Tanner till the evening. But then what?

Savannah darted into the kitchen, snatched the juice from Charity's hand, downed it in one gulp and headed for the back door, calling, "Don't forget the barn dance at Thistledown."

Charity ran after her sister. "Dance? What dance?"

Savannah paused by her Cavalier and kicked a loose hubcap back into place. "Nathan's throwing a prewedding get-together. Isn't he the greatest! We'll have fun, and I'll finally get a chance to talk with

Tanner.'' She winked at Charity. ''Since you've been keeping him all to yourself.''

Savannah drove off in a cloud of dust and oil-burning exhaust and Charity gazed at the retreating car. She'd wondered what to do that night and now she knew. *Keep Tanner away from that dance.* ''Why does there have to be a dance?''

''What dance?'' Patience asked as she came up beside her, dragging brush half her size.

''Guess I'm not the only one out of the loop. Nathan's throwing it over at Thistledown. Tonight.'' She nodded at the brush. ''What's that?''

''*Verbascum thapsus.* Mullein. For coughs. Mama needed some.'' Patience grinned. ''How's the Enthralling Tanner Plan coming? You going to enthrall him at the dance? That should be interesting since you've never been to a dance, have you?''

''Once.'' In junior high, when she helped serve punch rather than be a wallflower. ''Keep it down.''

''Tanner's not here.''

''You'd be surprised where that man shows up. And as for the enthralling…it's coming along.''

She glanced at Charity's jeans. ''Well, you're not doing much of anything in those. Do you even own a dress?''

Charity grinned and winked. ''No, but Savannah does. We're about the same size.''

Patience laughed and eyed Charity's chest. ''Not

everywhere. The waist might fit, but how do you intend to fill out the front?''

''We can trade you in for a brother, you know. It's not too late.''

Patience laughed again and walked to the house, dribbling *verbas* something after her. ''Oh, yes, it is.''

Nothing like a sibling to lay the facts out plain and clear whether you wanted to hear them or not. But what the heck was she going to do about them?

Later that evening, when everyone else had gone to the dance, Charity stood in the middle of Savannah's closet with two questions still hounding her. The first was how to keep Tanner and Savannah apart. She could keep Tanner away from the dance altogether, or—if that didn't work—keep him too busy to get to Savannah. That would mean dancing and flirting and whatever else it took to keep Tanner occupied.

Trouble was, when other girls were learning the finer points of keeping a man occupied, she'd been mucking stalls and memorizing bloodlines. Which brought her to the second problem.

She studied the contents of the closet—fashion mecca of the South, wooing central—and stripped to her underwear. She stuffed her bra with tissues. Where was the Wonderbra fairy when she needed her? Then she cranked up the music on the radio to drown out any doubts she had about all this. She snatched a glass of wine Savannah had left on her dresser and gulped.

Relax, she ordered herself. *Forget horses. Think sexy, think mysterious, think womanly. Forget impossible.* But she needed to hurry, the dance had already started. She practiced a swing step from an Elvis movie and kicked over a lamp. She twirled the way Baby had done in *Dirty Dancing* and knocked a pile of magazines.

Maybe she should just aim for graceful and work up to sexy, mysterious and womanly. She closed her eyes, tipped her chin, poised her wineglass elegantly aloft as she arched her tissue-enhanced chest and gyrated her hips—what hips?—across the room.

"Charity?"

"Tanner?" Her eyes flew open, the glass flipped into the air and she snatched two magazines from the floor and placed them in strategic places…mostly to conceal the tissue.

His eyes rounded. Red inched up his neck. "Uh…uh, Savannah sent me to get you because she wanted you at the dance and knew you wouldn't come or even answer the door because you're not the partying type. Said you were up here cleaning her room."

"Does this look like a maid's outfit?"

His left brow arched. "Depends on the maid."

"*Out!*"

"I'm going, I'm going. I'll wait for you down-stairs."

TANNER TURNED FROM the room as the door slammed shut behind him, rattling every pane of glass in the house. Desire settled in his groin. What was wrong with him? It wasn't as if he'd never seen a woman in her underwear before. And what was with those tissues? He'd never seen so *much* of Charity MacKay at one time…*and he really liked what he'd seen.*

Dammit. He was here to save his brother, not to salivate over Charity in her underwear. It must be that Alaskan man/woman ratio thing hassling him again.

Tanner clambered down the bare wooden steps and headed for the kitchen. Food. He yanked opened the fridge to the promised land. Corn bread, potato salad with a sprinkle of paprika, green beans with little pieces of ham.

He sampled the bread. Ecstasy. No thoughts of Charity…except for her soft hair. He reached for a drumstick. No one could eat Mama Kay's fried chicken and think of anything else…except Charity's soft skin and sweet womanly fragrance.

"Least you could do is eat at the table and save our electric bill."

Busted. He pulled his head from the fridge and faced Charity. "You're   probably…probably…"

Probably something. He couldn't remember what he intended to say. What happened to the hay usually tangled in her hair? No horse drool on her shoulder? Sandals? Pink toenails? Where were her old boots? He took two more bites of corn bread, but it didn't deter his fascination with Charity one lick. He mumbled, "We better get going. Savannah will wonder what happened to—"

"How much did you talk to Savannah? What did she say? What did *you* say?"

He shrugged. "She told me that I wasn't to leave here without you, and when I get back she wants to know about Alaska."

Charity twisted a lock of hair that curled by her ear and nibbled her bottom lip. Her full, pink, very-tempting bottom lip. Maybe he should try the potato salad.

"Have any plans on how to stop the wedding?" she asked.

He wiped his hands on a paper towel and tossed it into the garbage along with the demolished chicken leg. He leaned against the chipped counter. "I have an idea for tonight."

She folded her arms and leaned against the counter, too. "Doesn't this bother you just a little bit? It's manipulative and sneaky."

"Like I said, I'm not manipulating anyone. And I am not sneaking anything. Tonight I'm just going to get Savannah to dance. That's it."

"Didn't know Nathan hated dancing enough to call off his engagement over it."

"Not just *dancing,* dancing, but dancing on top of the bar. Savannah used to do it all the time at parties. She loved it. Nathan, on the other hand, hates a scene. Loathes being the center of attention. When his horses win races, he won't even go to the winner's circle."

"Doesn't sound like a great plan to me. We should stay here so you can think of something else. What if Savannah's dancing-on-the-bar-days are over? Ever consider that? She's older now. More sophisticated. We have bar*stools* and she doesn't even *sit* on them."

His grin gave way to laughter. "If Savannah lives to be a hundred, her dancing days still won't be over."

Besides, they couldn't stay here because he'd never be able to keep his hands off Charity. Nope, they needed lots and lots of people around. "We'd better go."

"But…but…"

Ten minutes later as he stood at the entrance of the barn-turned-dance pavilion with Charity, he knew this was the perfect setting to get Savannah going, *and* to keep his thoughts off Charity. Paper lanterns swung gently from strands of suspended lights, bails of hay served as tables, chairs and the bar. A great band fiddled away. Dancers crowded the floor. The horses had obviously been relocated to other residences for the occasion.

"Okay," Charity said over the music, "now what?"

"Now you get the band to play something wild and reckless while I—"

"Me?"

"You *are* a part of this, right?"

She nodded and he continued. "While I remind Savannah of the good-old dancing days, when a gang of us would sneak off to..." Charity's brows raised to her hairline.

"Not sneak, exactly. More like not tell anyone where we were going."

She rolled her eyes.

"Okay, we were sneaky as hell. And I'm sure being the big sister and trying to keep Savannah out of trouble and not worry your mother into an early grave was the stuff nightmares are made of. But tonight all that's important is to get Savannah on that bar and to show Nate he has nightmares of his very own in store if he marries her."

Tanner nodded toward the band. "It's show time."

He watched Charity start off, then rounded his way through the crowd to Savannah, who sat with a group of high school friends. She spied him and met him halfway across the room, looping her arm around his waist.

"Why, there you are, you bad boy. You were gone much too long. I see you got Charity." She smiled and gestured toward the bar. "Doesn't Nathan look handsome as all get-out tonight? Let's join him and you can tell me about Alaska."

The music suddenly turned to hip-hop. Good old dependable Charity. Then he caught sight of her heading in the direction of the bar and realized there was not one thing old about her. She was dazzling.

He said to Savannah, "I'll tell you all about Alaska later, but this is your engagement party. All your friends are here, and just listen to that music." He nodded at the band. "Reminds me of the times the gang would sneak up to the lake, go skinny-dipping and dance like crazy."

Her eyes brightened. "Gee, that seems a zillion years ago."

"Doesn't have to be. Least, the dancing part." He tipped his head toward the dance floor. "Well?"

She shot him a hundred-kilowatt smile. "You are right as rain, Tanner Davenport. I'm feeling the need to shake my booty. Don't think Nathan's ever seen me dance, I mean *really* dance and kick up my heels."

She bebopped her way to the middle of the barn and Tanner made for Nathan and Charity, feeling downright pleased with himself. He said to Nate, "Well, look at that. Your fiancé sure can move."

"Yeah." Nathan's voice was throaty, sort of a croak. His eyes never left Savannah as her golden hair swayed, her arms waved and her body twirled to the music. She kicked her red sandals into the air, making guests cheer and gather 'round clapping to the beat and encouraging her.

Perspiration dotted Nathan's forehead. A vein at his left temple throbbed, his eyes glazed. Was he breathing? Charity snagged two beers and handed him one. "You need this." She looked back at Savannah and gulped the other beer. "*I* need this."

Savannah boogied onto a hay bale, took the red sash from her dress and swung it over her head. The crowd cheered and Tanner said to Charity, "This is great. Perfect. I'm brilliant. Look at Nathan. He's stunned. Going to have a stroke right here in his own barn."

Savannah kicked and whirled and stepped up onto the bar. The crowd cheered again and she looped the sash around the back of Nathan's neck, pulling him closer to her as she danced. She bent to him, her face to his, gazing into his eyes and giving him a view of cleavage only husbands, or near-husbands, should have.

Tanner grinned and said to Charity, "My brother will never forget this night."

Nathan's eyes widened to the size of softballs and Savannah ran her fingers through his immaculate hair, then mussed it in all directions. Still dancing, she un-did the top three buttons of his shirt and she gave him a big, wet kiss. The crowd went wild, Tanner con-gratulated himself on a job magnificently well done, and Nathan leaped onto the bar with Savannah.

Huh?

The crowd screamed, the music blared louder and

Tanner choked. "Wait a minute. *What's he doing?* Nathan doesn't dance."

Charity swayed to the sexy rhythm, grinning ear-to-ear, clapping to the beat. "Guess Nathan doesn't know that. Never seen him like this. Doubt if anyone on the Ridge has. He sure is having fun. Chalk one up for Cupid."

She turned to Tanner, eyes shining, face radiant, and he was sure he'd never seen *her* like this, either. Did she have to look at him that way, as though she was happy to be with him? Right now he sure felt happy to be with her even though his great plan had just blown up in his face.

Dang it all. Cupid was working overtime tonight and Tanner had no one to blame but himself.

Chapter Four

The next morning Charity hit the barns extra early. It was a beautiful day. Birds sang, trees bloomed and she'd had a great time last night. Except for Tanner walking in on her in Savannah's bedroom. She laughed to herself. Who was she kidding? That was the most fun of all. The expression on his face was priceless, the hunger in his eyes memorable. First time she'd ever done that to a man. Too bad he lived three thousand miles away. Then again, if he lived closer what would she do about it? *Nothing.* There wasn't time for both Tanner and the farm.

She mixed malt with oats and walked past the other stalls to Silver Bell's. "Here you go, girl," she whispered. She took a brush from the wall. "This will make you feel better. I'll keep you inside today. Get you gussied up for spring and comb out some of that winter coat you're still carrying around."

The sound of footsteps on concrete came her way

and she looked up to see Tanner. "You talk to that horse like she understands every word."

"And you don't think she does?"

He chuckled softly. "Yeah, I'm sure she does."

Denim shirt open at the throat, thin lines at the corners of his eyes, hair mussed as if it refused to lie down... Strong. Male. A touch of awesome. She wished this assessment came from her horny state of spinsterhood, but it didn't. After listening to Tanner at the school, then at the library, she knew he was all that and more. Not that he boasted. That wasn't his style. "Are all bush pilots noisy as you?"

"Practice for keeping polar bears away." He stopped at the stall and took a knife from his pocket. He quartered an apple from a basketful of the horse treats.

"Polar bears are so cute, all soft and furry and white."

He grinned. "As long as they're on TV. You don't go near bears unless you have a death wish. But they are magnificent. Cranky and territorial as hell, but magnificent."

He cut himself a big chunk of apple and offered another to Silver Bell. "She sure likes apples."

"But she's not touching anything else. I think she just spit at her breakfast. Are you here to entertain me with bear stories or to feed my horse?"

He shared another quarter with Silver Bell. "To borrow some ground malt. Now two of Nathan's mares are off their feed. When Mama Kay was over with Puck she said it might encourage them to eat.''

He gave up the last slice then leaned against the stall, arms folded, driving Charity loony by doing absolutely nothing.

She nodded at a brush on the wall. ''Make yourself useful as well as ornamental, flyboy. This horse has two sides.'' And with Tanner buried behind a horse, there'd be a lot less of him to go loony over. ''I thought Mama lost interest in the horses a long time ago, but she checked on them for me, too.''

Tanner rolled his sleeves to the elbows. Did he have to expose more skin? That defeated the whole brushing-behind-the-horse idea. ''I wonder why the sudden interest now.''

He picked up the brush and went to work. ''I think she felt she let down the farm and the horses, so she was down on herself. Coming to the barns was too painful. But now the farm's on the mend and so is she. She and Puck have been spending a lot of time together.''

''They've been friends forever.''

Tanner laughed. He had a great laugh, the kind that made her happy just listening to it. ''Yeah, just friends.''

''What's that supposed to mean?''

''Puck didn't hang around your farm all these years, living over the garage, only to train horses. Hell, for a time there you didn't even have horses.''

"You're reading way too much into this friendship between Mama and Puck. He's part of the family, like a favorite uncle."

"Right."

And she *was* right, she felt sure of it. But now that Tanner's brain was homed in on romance, it seemed a good time to finesse a strategy about Savannah and Nathan's wedding. To make him see *they* were the ones who belonged together. Then she wouldn't have to spend eleven more days with him, trying to keep him and Savannah apart.

Why didn't the idea thrill her as much as she thought it would? She took in his strong shoulders as he brushed Silver Bell and instantly knew why. She liked spending time with him. Looked forward to him dropping in every day and spicing things up. Good and bad. Not only was he mouthwateringly gorgeous, he was loyal and protective, too. It had been a long time since she'd met someone as protective as herself.

Heck, that's what had brought them together in the first place. She was protecting Savannah and he was protecting Nathan. Too bad *he* was so misguided.

He said, "You going to stand there gawking at me or brush Silver Bell?"

She blushed, feeling the heat pool in her cheeks. Dang. She started brushing, keeping her face turned away from Tanner. She certainly didn't need him thinking she *had been* gawking at him...even if she had. "About the wedding…what if Savannah and Nathan are meant to be and we louse it up?"

"What brought that on?"

"Mama and Puck. You seem to think *they* belong together, so why not Savannah and Nathan? And if they are meant to be together, we'll feel terrible about breaking them up. We'll need years of therapy to get over it. They probably don't have many therapists in Alaska and they're probably booked up forever with so many dark days. And Savannah and Nathan will be miserable and never talk to us again."

"I'm sure there are enough therapists in Alaska, not that I'll need one." He looked at her over Silver Bell's back. "I'm just watching out for Nate. I owe him. He always tried to smooth things out between me and Dad." An easy smile suddenly slid across his face. "Plus, Nate's one hell of a nice guy. I don't want him to get into something that will end in a mess, and that's what will happen if he and Savannah wed."

"But Savannah really loves Nathan. That's why she wants to marry him. It's not like he's spoiling her with big expensive gifts to turn her head. They truly get along well. Nathan dancing on the bar proved it. Ever consider that?"

"What I think is, my levelheaded brother dancing on that bar proved he's lost his ever-loving mind. This insane attraction between him and Savannah makes as much sense as this attraction between you and me.''

Tanner's head snapped up. Charity's jaw dropped. Their gazes locked tighter than a lid to a honey jar.

He looked at Charity across the back of Silver Bell. ''Not…not that I'm attracted. Or you're attracted. Or we're attracted.''

Was he conjugating a verb or what? Was that perspiration on his forehead?

''I was only making a point, that's all…about people not fitting together because of things in their lives keeping them apart and—''

A car horn blasted loud enough to rattle the rafters. Charity let out a chuckle and said, ''Tell me, oh Swami of the High Skies, how much did you pay that person out there to show up at this moment?''

Whoever it was, Charity didn't know whether to bless him for interrupting a sticky situation or to wring his neck for the same reason. What *had* Tanner been thinking that had made him say what he had?

TANNER WIPED HIS shirtsleeve across his sweaty brow. *Saved by the horn.* What the hell had made him say he was attracted to Charity? Then he considered that shining red hair, those alluring lips that had driven him nuts last night, and those green eyes, full of life and energy. Charity MacKay had a slice of tenacity a yard wide and a mile long right up her spine.

Attracted to her? What man wouldn't be?

The horn blasted again and Charity put down her brush and headed for the entrance. "We better see what's going on out there or they'll be honking till midnight."

He followed Charity out of the stable, both of them quiet as tombstones. What could he say? *I apologize for the attack of temporary insanity that seems to be running through my family these days?*

Tanner halted behind her at the entrance as Savannah pulled her new cherry-red BMW convertible to a gravel-spitting stop by the water trough. She spread her arms wide in the air. "Isn't this the greatest car ever? Whoopee!"

Charity smacked her palm to her forehead. "What are you doing? We can't afford this car. We can't even afford the tires on it. Take it back. Hurry."

Savannah beamed. "Don't go getting your panties in a twist, sister dear. Sweet Nathan gave it to me. It's a wedding present. Have you ever seen anything so awesome?"

She revved the engine. "I've got to get back to Nathan, then I have to get to work. We're doing a road trip to Lexington tonight to see how this little treasure performs."

She patted the steering wheel. "Nathan sent me here to pick up that malt stuff." She eyed Tanner. "Says he wants it now. Another horse isn't looking so good and two ready to foal. Poor Nathan, he's going to worry himself into the grave over those horses.''

Charity shook her head. ''Some gift.''

''We're getting married, Charity. This is *fun*. Marrying is supposed to be fun. Can I have that malt now?''

Charity turned to Tanner. ''How about helping me?''

''In a minute.''

She looked at Savannah, then back to Tanner. ''I'll be right back. In a flash. Talk about...the weather.'' She scurried into the barn.

Tanner rested his arm on the top of the windshield. A BMW convertible? No wonder Savannah wanted to marry Nathan. He said, ''Just like old times, huh?''

''Old times?'' She shook her head. ''I wasn't engaged to Nathan then.''

''I mean the joy-riding, the excitement, the fun.'' He patted the car. ''What about going flying with me tomorrow? Remember when we used to do that and talk about all the places we wanted to visit, the adventures we wanted to have?''

Her whole face lit up. This was a good thing. The wedding would be history by noon; look out Indiana Jones, here comes Savannah MacKay.

''You're going to get the biplane out of the barn? Nathan's kept it covered for so many years. I adore that plane.''

Tanner ran his hand around the back of his neck.

"Hadn't planned on dragging out the *Starduster*—" and all its memories "—but if you really want me to and it still runs, why the hell not?"

He grinned, suddenly not feeling as thrilled as he tried to appear. "See you tomorrow. Late afternoon?"

Charity came back with the powder and handed it to Savannah. "Here you are, you can go now." She looked from Tanner to her sister. "What did you two talk about?"

Savannah laughed. "Tanner's going to take me flying." She drove off, waving, sending critters diving for cover.

Tanner nodded at the retreating splash of red. "Tell me again about no expensive gifts and not being spoiled?"

"It's a wedding gift. Nathan's allowed to give her a wedding gift, just like she said."

"He *is* spoiling her rotten. Big fancy wedding, new car. He can give her anything she wants, and he probably will."

"She loves him."

"Or does she love his money and what he can offer her? Her life hasn't been too cushy around here." He waved his hand, taking in the house that needed repairs, the rusted car, the cracked driveway.

"Oh, I get it now." Charity put her hands on her hips. "You don't want Savannah to marry Nathan because you don't think she's good enough for him. That's the whole problem, isn't it?"

"Huh? What do you mean? That's not what I said at all. Spoiling and *good enough* are two different things."

"Not if they both center around money." Her green eyes sparked and her lush lips tightened to a thin line. "You think the lowly MacKays aren't good enough for the high-and-mighty Davenports because we're not members of the Horseman's Club and we don't have box seats at the Derby and—"

"Who cares?"

"You do." She tossed her head. "We did have all those things once, Tanner Davenport, and we will again. I swear it."

He stood his ground. "You know I'm not impressed with that stuff and neither is Nathan. I merely said that—"

"You're a snob." She took a step toward him.

He glanced down at his worn jeans and denim shirt and remembered the hole in his left sock. "Me?"

"You think you're better than my family because we were poor, nearly lost everything and even wore hand-me-downs. You don't want your brother having anything to do with the MacKays, much less marry one."

"*Enough.*" He snatched her up into his arms, surprising the heck out of her and himself, as well. He held her tight as she pushed at his chest, but he wouldn't let her go till he had his say. "Hear this, Kentucky Girl. Life dumps on everybody one way or another. It's how you get over it that counts, and you haven't gotten over one damn thing no matter how many barns you build or horses you have.''

''Easy for a rich boy who's had everything handed to him to say.''

''You're pissed off because you work nonstop and life's passing you by at warp speed.''

Then he kissed her. Hot. Wild. Furiously mad and totally delicious. ''That's because I admire what you've done.'' I like the way you feel in my arms and I like kissing you and… ''But you have a chip on your shoulder the size of North America and you're *not* taking it out on me.''

He dropped her butt-first into the trough, splashing water everywhere as her arms and legs flailed about. ''And that's because you need to cool off before you say any more stupid things.''

Hell, he's the one who needed a dousing of cold water.

Charity stood, stumbling, dripping water, wiping wet hair from her face. Her eyes shot green sparks at him. Was that steam curling from her ears? Or was the steam coming from him?

''I'll get you for this.''

''You'll have to dry out first. You and your opinion are all wet and you know it.'' He turned for his truck.

''Blast you, Tanner Davenport. You're not going to get the last word!''

Water hit his back, drenching him from his neck to his knees.

He spun around and faced Charity, eyes lit with fire, bucket in hand, smile of satisfaction on her lips. He took a step toward her and stopped dead. If he took one more step, he wouldn't stop at all. He'd snatch her back in his arms, head into the barn and kiss her till they both collapsed of exhaustion. She had more spunk, more grit, more natural beauty—in and out of a water trough—than any woman he'd ever met.

Kissing her again would be like pouring gas on a smoldering fire and he didn't need any explosions right now. Especially from a horse farmer tied to the land, who thought adventure was painting her fences white instead of brown. Dammit all. He needed to get back to Alaska—get back to his piloting business and adventurous life and to forget about Charity MacKay.

He turned for the truck again with, "Keep cool, Tanner Davenport," ringing in his ears and knowing that when it came to Charity MacKay he'd never feel cool again.

THE FIRST RAYS of light peeked over the six white-and-green copulas of Thistledown stables as Tanner headed for a small barn some distance beyond the others. His boots crushed gravel as spring fog billowed over acres of rolling bluegrass and endless fences. Dogwoods and rhododendron scented the air, birds sang for breakfast, vermin scurried in the brush. Then a vision of Charity MacKay bobbing in the water trough, soaked to the skin and feisty as bacon on a hot griddle, flashed through his mind.

He'd been having these visions of her all night. Not so much the soaked or the feisty ones, but the kissing ones sure as hell kept him awake. Charity was all fire and emotion. All woman. Now what the hell was he going to do about her?

Nothing, if he had an ounce of sense. One—and only one—kiss was his quota. He needed a plan, a How Not to Fall for Charity Plan, because that's exactly where he was headed. Okay, he had to spend time with her to break up Nathan's engagement, but he'd simply make that time as short as possible. If he wasn't with Charity, he couldn't kiss her and he couldn't fall for her.

Good plan. Now he could concentrate on taking Savannah flying this afternoon.

The barn door creaked when he pulled it open and he peered into the shadows at the draped gray tarp. He snagged an end, then tugged it off, revealing propeller, cockpit, double wings and tail. He'd bought the *Starduster* with his own money, fixed her up and painted her yellow with navy trim. He could still hear his father yelling at him to get back to the horses and forget the damn plane. This was a horse farm, not a damn airport. He had work to do and why couldn't he be more like Nathan...?

Tanner paused for a second. Had he and his father ever agreed on anything? Yeah, him getting the hell off the Ridge. And, Charity MacKay. A woman they had never discussed was the one thing they had in common…besides a dented chin.

Tanner flipped the light switch and shed his jacket, enjoying the morning chill. A touch of Alaska? He smiled at the thought of Grady Donavon—best partner ever, and pictured glaciers, snowcapped mountains, thundering waterfalls tumbling into crystal-clear lakes and mosquitoes that could carry off small children. No place was perfect.

He rolled his sleeves, pulled a KitKat from his pocket and munched on it as he inspected the plane from wings to wheels and everything in between. He added oil, filled tires, greased fittings, checked hoses, then stood back and admired the first plane he ever owned. "Not too bad for an old gal."

"That's what I say every morning when I look in the mirror."

Tanner cut his eyes to the door and Charity framed in the entrance. "Thirty-two isn't exactly old."

"It's no spring chicken, either."

"Depends on the chicken." Nice silhouette. Nice shape. He remembered how she felt in his arms and his insides clenched into a hard knot.

She walked in and handed him a wicker basket covered with a red-checked napkin.

"Fried arsenic?"

"Blueberry muffins. I need you to fly me to Davey's Junction."

"You need a favor from a snob?"

She shrugged. "Okay, so you're not a snob. Your hair's too long. They'd never let you in the Horseman's Club with that shirt. And you eat out of the refrigerator."

"Is that an apology?"

"Close as you'll get since you nearly drowned me. One of Mama's friends over at the junction has two horses not eating at all. Mama made a yeast concoction that keeps toxins from being digested and that might help. I need to get it to her ASAP."

Tanner leaned against the fuselage, taking her in, catching a whiff of her unique scent—Kentucky spring and wildflowers all rolled into one. He looked at the basket. He should think about those muffins and not the gal who brought them. Or the gal he kissed last night.

He pulled a muffin from the basket and bit. "Maybe," he said around a mouthful of instant heaven, "she needs to call the vet."

Charity gave him a don't-be-stupid look. "Of course she called the vet. Everyone's calling vets. Vets are running all over Kentucky like ants over a picnic, but they don't have any answers and horses are getting real skinny."

She was making jokes, but he noticed a hint of worry in her eyes. He stopped mid-chew. He didn't want Charity worrying. He put the muffin back into the basket. She'd done more than enough of that in her life. "What's going on, Charity?"

She rubbed her forehead. "Beats the heck out of me, but something's not right, and it seems to be getting worse. Sick horses aren't uncommon, but this rash of sick horses we have now is." She huffed a sigh. "So, you going to fly me or what? Davey's Junction is almost three hours by car and maybe a half hour as the crow flies."

"And I'm the crow." A shaft of sunlight fell across her face, making her more beautiful than ever. This wasn't part of his Not Falling for Charity Plan. Hell, according to the plan, she wasn't supposed to be here at all. He gripped the basket with both hands to keep from touching her. He really wanted to touch her. "You could have left earlier this morning, you know."

"Yeah, well I'm asking now."

"I'm supposed to take Savannah flying this afternoon. It's her short day at the office."

"She can't make it. One more fitting for her dress. A little wrinkle in the back that I found. I'm very good at finding wrinkles. I knew you'd be here, so I told Mama we'd deliver the feed."

"At this rate I'll never get Savannah flying and the wedding will go off without a hitch."

She tisked. "Hey, something will come up. I'll help."

"Like you have so far?"

"I'm thinking, I'm thinking. You haven't done such a great job, either."

He looked back to the basket. "And you really expect me to fly to Davey's Junction for muffins?"

"How about for a fat lip if you say no." Charity folded her arms and winked. "Besides, there's apple pie waiting for us."

"Pie? Help me push the plane out and we'll fuel up and be on our way."

"WAIT." CHARITY'S heart skipped a beat and she could feel little beads of sweat pop out all over her body.

"Now what? You're kidding about the pie. That's it, isn't it?"

"What…what about your other plane, the Cessna, the one with a top. Tops on airplanes are a real good idea, Tanner. Keep everybody inside from falling out."

"I've worked half the day on the *Starduster*. It'll be a good test to see how she runs."

"*Test?*" Her eyes bulged.

"Besides, biplanes are more fun."

She swallowed a whine. Maybe she should tell him heights weren't exactly her thing. But then maybe he wouldn't fly her and his date with Savannah would happen after all. She forced a chuckle. "Yeah, what was I thinking? Silly me. Biplanes are blooming terrific.''

A half hour later she was headed skyward, white-knuckled, leaving safe green pastures behind. She felt sicker than she'd been ten years ago when she'd ridden the Ferris wheel at the Kentucky State Fair.

"Isn't this great?" Tanner called from the back. "Look at the silver in the trees. I don't remember seeing that before."

Wind twisted her hair. It would take a month to get the knots out. She sure as heck wasn't about to look at any trees; she'd keep her eyes on the sky. As long as she didn't look down she could pretend this little scene was simply blue paint on a wall and she was sitting in front of a big fan...until the plane dropped, then rose, sending her stomach to her throat.

She glanced back at Tanner, wide-eyed, sure her hair now stood straight on end and was perfectly white. "What was that?" she yelled over the drone of the engine.

"Turbulence." He hitched his chin to the side and she noticed a gray puff of cotton. A storm? Oh, no. No, no. Not a storm. *Mother have mercy.* She didn't mind dying so much—that would happen sooner or later—it was dropping from the sky like a giant bucket of cement that scared the spit out of her.

This was her punishment for calling Tanner a snob and for all the lies she'd told him. If he ever found out and if God happened to be keeping track of them... Oh, boy!

Tanner tapped her back and she turned around. He pointed down. They buzzed a water tower with Davey's Junction written in faded black letters. She swallowed a burp and yelled, "Look for a red windmill that way." She pointed west.

The plane banked in that direction, getting lower to the earth—lower was good as long as it happened gradually. They circled the windmill, lower still, trees skimming underneath the plane, then next to it. Then they were bumping over pasture and coming to a halt. She unhooked her harness, scrambled over the side, slid to the ground, falling face-first into the grass. She kissed it.

"Are you all right?" Tanner knelt on one knee, turning her over. She flipped onto her back, arms and legs spread like a big X, trying to catch her breath and waiting for the world to stop spinning.

"If you had waited a minute, I would have helped you down and—"

She threw her arms around his neck and held tight, pulling him off balance and collapsing him on top of her. "Oh, thank you, thank you, thank you for getting us down. I wasn't ready to die."

He went completely still. Was he *dead?* "Tanner?"

She relaxed her grip, letting him push up on his elbows. He gazed down at her, his eyes brown as the finest Kentucky bourbon. The little cleft in his chin and his mouth inches from hers, his breath feathering her face.

"You want to tell me what's going on here? I'm not complaining, mind you, though it's a bit unexpected."

"I—I hate flying. *Really* hate flying. I'm…grateful for being on the ground. That's all, nothing more." Although with Tanner on top and the rise and fall of his steely chest against her breasts and his hips snuggled against hers, this was not a *that's all* situation no matter how much she tried to convince herself or him that it was.

He raised his brow. "Is this how you thank all pilots that bring you back to earth?"

She swallowed, trying to lie very still and to not move her hips or any other suggestive parts and not get excited. This situation had excitement written all over it. "There have never been any other pilots."

"Yoo-hoo," came from the barn some feet away. "Charity? Is that you on the ground under that young man? Sure hope I'm interrupting something good. The Ridge could do with a bit of gossip. Been too darn quiet around here. Everybody's behaved themselves lately. What's the fun in that?"

Tanner pushed himself up and Charity scrambled after him. They both stood, brushing themselves off, avoiding each other's gaze. Charity pointed to the plane. "No gossip here. I sort of fell when I got out.

Slid from the plane like a snake on a wet rock. Tanner came to see if I was okay.''

Alvena Cahill smoothed back her curly salt-and-pepper hair and looked from Charity to Tanner. Her gray eyes flickered with interest as she smiled. "Well, now, I'm sure he did. Very gentlemanly of him to come over and take care of you like that."

She looked at Tanner. "Welcome home, boy. I suppose you're here for Nathan's wedding, and a jim-dandy one it's going to be, too. Whole town's twitter-pated. Bought myself a new dress over in Louisville."

Tanner shrugged. "Nathan and Savannah aren't exactly the perfect match, so it wouldn't surprise me if the wedding was called off and—"

Alvena threw back her head and laughed. "Perfect match? Since when does that have anything to do with falling in love? Love happens when it's good and ready to, and there's not one single thing anyone can do to stop it. Now where's my medicine, so you two can get back to falling out of airplanes?" She winked. "Fell out of a few things myself when I was young." She laughed again. "And even some when not so young."

Charity handed Alvena the package. "Don't add sugar, but use a little white corn syrup to tempt the horses into eating. The yeast mixture should make them feel better in a day or so. Let Mama know how it's working."

Alvena's smile faded. "I'm banking on it working

real good. The vets around here are calling in some experts at the university to figure out this problem we've got brewing. Trouble is, we don't have time for their figuring. We got problems now. Mares are getting ready to foal, and if they aren't in good health, things could get mighty complicated." Her smile kicked up a notch and she patted the bag. "But I'm sure this will take care of things. Your mama's the best. She's the one who these vets need to talk to. I baked you one of my Dutch apple pies to take with you."

Alvena headed back to the barn as Tanner glanced at the sky. "Well, Kentucky Girl, are you ready to go? It's clouding up. If you want a smooth ride, we better move on."

Charity looked at gray puffs overhead. Her stomach lurched and her knees went to jelly. "See you around, flyboy. I'm walking. You can drop my pie off later. Thanks for the lift."

Chapter Five

Tanner snagged her arm as she strode past him on her way back to MacKay Farms. "Wait up, Kentucky Girl. If you try to walk home, you won't get there till next week, and what makes you think Alvena's pie is yours?" He hitched his chin at the biplane. "You know the real reason you don't like to fly, don't you?"

"The pie is mine and I don't like flying because I'm suspended *in* air *by* air and that makes no sense at all?"

"Not quite. You don't like it because someone else is doing the flying." He gave her a smug look. "You're at someone else's mercy, and you can't stand the thought. It's a control thing."

"That's ridiculous."

He arched his brow, looking every inch the confident rogue in faded jeans and mussed hair. She doubted if any male on earth fit the part as well as

Tanner Davenport. Maybe because he'd been a rogue his whole life.

"All right, it's not ridiculous. I'm a little controlling."

He studied her through half-closed lids.

"Okay, I'm a lot controlling. Happy? But I still hate heights."

"Come on, sissy pants, fly with me. I haven't lost a passenger yet."

"Sissy pants? You called me 'sissy pants'?"

He grinned and folded his arms. They crossed his very muscular chest, which had pressed against her minutes ago and made her hotter than a pump handle in July.

"Got to think of some way to get you in that plane. Thought maybe a dare would do it."

"Since Puck's driving Mama to Louisville today, I'll bum the old truck Alvena has around back and return it tomorrow."

He made chicken sounds. She hated chicken sounds. She hated flying even more. She gave him a superior look. "Nothing you can do or say will change my mind. I am not flying in that…that contraption."

Minutes later she sat in Alvena's spluttering truck as Tanner stared at her through the open window.

"So it runs a little rough and has a few minor idiosyncrasies."

"Like not getting out of third gear and no head-lights?" he said, grinning.

Did he have to grin? She couldn't think when he did that…except about the grin. And maybe his eyes. She thought a lot about his terrific brown eyes. And his hair. She bet it would feel great running through her fingers. Then there was that kiss. She'd never forget Tanner kissing her if she lived to be a hundred. 'Course she'd never forget him dropping her in that trough, either.

There wouldn't be other kisses. Getting involved with a man who made his home on an iceberg was nuts. She and Tanner had nothing in common—not where they lived, not their stand on this wedding, not what they intended to do with the rest of their lives. *Except there was that darn kiss, which they had in common big-time.*

She turned back to the steering wheel and away from Tanner and his grin and memories of the kiss. "I'll be home before dark. If I do have problems I can *walk* away from them and not have to wish I could grow wings. I have a cell phone and I know every farm between here and home, so there's nothing to worry about."

"Bet that cell phone works real great in these mountains, and think of all the land separating the farms around here. What if this hunk of junk conks out in between?" He raked his hand through his hair and shook his head. "I'm not making any impression on you at all, am I?"

Ha. She looked at him and smiled. Darn it, she shouldn't have looked.

"Guess this makes you a full-fledged member of the if-God-wanted-us-to-fly-he'd-have-given-us-wings club."

"Amen." Least she wouldn't be with Tanner and she could get herself under control and figure out how not to be so affected by him before they met up again. She could also try real hard to forget about that kiss.

She slid the truck into gear, gave Tanner a little finger wave goodbye and chugged off into the hazy afternoon.

TANNER HAD NO TROUBLE spotting the faded red truck meandering along the curvy back roads. He'd followed her by air for the past two hours, telling himself this was stupid, dumb, idiotic. Nothing would happen to Charity MacKay. She knew these roads like she knew the bloodline and birth order of every horse on the Ridge, but he just couldn't let her fend for herself in that pitiful excuse of a truck. He had to keep an eye on her. Besides, she took his pie.

He did a wide circle, enjoying the warmth of the late-afternoon sun when it peeked through the clouds, the pink and purple wildflowers, the budding trees surrounded by lighter shades of grass. Funny how he never noticed the different color from the ground, only from the air. He swooped low over Thistledown, canvassing the farm front to back from the big red-brick house and stables on one end to the original Davenport cabin his granddaddy built at the far end. Tanner did a barrel role, a salute to granddad, a gutsy man. The engine missed.

Now what? Tanner checked gauges and listened to the steady rhythm, except it wasn't so steady. *Hellfire and damnation.* If he wasn't running out of gas, something else had to flare up. Fuel pump? He'd checked the damn fuel pump. Twice. The engine spluttered again and died. *Full engine failure.* And he'd been worried about Charity's damn truck breaking down. The gods of irony, sarcasm and mockery were, no doubt, laughing their butts off.

He banked to the left, thankful he was in a biplane that could glide, and searched for terrain more hospitable for an emergency landing than a hill and a hollow. He spied a pasture. Short, but the best thing available. He banked again, eating up speed, letting the plane slow so as not to run out of pasture, but not slow enough to lose control. The wheels touched; the three-point landing into the soft grass rattled every bone in his body. He applied the brakes and the *Starduster* coasted to a stop short of a tree line. He puffed out a breath of air and gazed skyward, offering thanks.

In reply he got a clap of thunder in the distance, echoing through the mountains, telling him he was screwed. The gods were not letting up. He looked west and spied a line of black clouds. The front was moving in faster than he'd expected. He tossed the tie-downs from the plane, then the chalks to keep the *Starduster* in place. But what the hell would he tie it to?

"See, see."

Charity? He spun around and there she stood. Beautiful and windblown and looking like the queen of Flying is for Dummies.

She spread her arm wide. "What did I tell you about nothing keeping you up in that sky except air?"

"Where'd you come from? How'd you know where I was?"

Her eyes rounded. "Good gravy, Davenport. You've been circling over me like some vulture."

"Try guardian angel."

"Ha! Angels don't fall out of the sky. I heard your plane suddenly sound as if it had a two-pack-a-day habit, then die. Figured you had to be around here somewhere and since I didn't see a big ball of fire, I figured you survived whatever happened."

The color suddenly drained from her face and she grabbed the front of his shirt in her fists. Her body was close to his, her voice low and ragged. "Don't *ever* do that again. You scared the hell out of me, Tanner."

Raw emotion sparked in her eyes. Trees, grass, insects seemed to freeze in place. Her hands felt warm, secure, caring. His heart skipped a beat and he swallowed hard. Been a long time since somebody besides Nate cared. "Yeah, scared the hell out of me, too."

She grinned. Her grin seemed forced, killing the moment, putting their relationship back on shallow ground and she let go of his shirt as if it were made of hot coals. This was good. Shallow he could handle, and from the looks of it, so could Charity. They didn't know what to do with that raw emotion stuff. Such as the kissing. That really added to the problem. There wasn't one thing shallow about that kiss. How could two people be attracted and have so little in common?

She put her hands to her hips. "So what do you have in mind, Mr. Top Gun?"

He thought, *Not get involved with Charity MacKay and get my sorry butt back to Alaska.* He said, "Drive the truck over here. Then we'll pull the plane into the trees and tie her down. If a wind gets under the wings she'll somersault and it's goodbye plane. It looks like a storm's heading our way."

"We pushed the plane before. Can't we do the same now?"

"Grass is too high. She won't roll worth a damn."

He followed Charity back to the truck parked on the roadside. He slid in beside her, keeping distance between himself and her tempting body. She put the bag-of-bolts into gear and headed for the *Starduster*.

"Since my truck is saving your plane," she said

as they bounced over the gully and into the pasture, "you owe my truck an apology."

"It's not *your* truck, and I don't apologize to inanimate objects."

"Oh, boy. You just had to go and say something stupid like that, didn't you? Bad karma, Tanner. If you don't treat things right, they poop out on you. Like getting your car washed. Doesn't your car always run better after you wash it? That makes for good karma."

She pulled up to the *Starduster*. He threw the tiedowns and chalks into the bed, tied the plane to the hitch and got back in the truck. Charity started up and he cautioned, "Not too fast. Can you help me tie her to the trees before the storm sets in?"

"I'd be glad to. But then what will we do?"

"Drive home and get my tools to fix the plane."

"Sounds like a plan, except for one little thing." She pulled up to the trees.

"And that would be?"

She nodded at the dashboard. "We're out of gas."

"Gas? Impossible." He tapped the glass over the gauge. "It showed full when you left. I checked."

"Well, it isn't now." She gave him a superior look. "You should have apologized."

"The gauge was probably stuck. *Damn.* I should have known. Nothing else works right on this thing." He raked his hair, thunder boomed, a fat raindrop hit the windshield. "When we don't show up, Mama Kay will call Alvena and they'll realize something's happened and come after us.''

"You *have* been away for a while. What will happen is, Alvena will tell Mama about you and me falling out of the plane and into the grass. Mama will tell Alvena we were in town together, and they'll both think we're off somewhere playing kissy-face and not worry one lick.''

She heaved a deep sigh. "We're going to be here till this blasted storm blows over. Then we can walk home. It will only take us an hour or so if we cut across the hills to Thistledown on the other side.''

She glanced at the sky. "Storm's just getting some teeth now and it's getting late. We're going to be out in this mess all night. Hope Mama and Puck mind the horses.''

"You know they will.'' Thunder rolled, winds kicked up, drops of water plopped onto Tanner's head. He touched his wet hair and frowned. "It leaks.''

"You didn't apologize.''

"We're on the backside of Thistledown. There's a cabin there, we'll make for that. It can't be worse than this hunk of rust.'' Two more drops hit his head.

She eyed the drops sliding down his forehead then onto his nose and said, "When we get to the cabin, I'll give you a lecture on karma. In the meantime, do us both a favor and keep all disparaging remarks about the cabin to yourself. I'd like for it to stay standing till this storm is over.''

The wind whipped around them as they got the tie-downs from the back and anchored the plane. Charity MacKay wasn't just beautiful—along with being a smart-ass—she was more capable than anyone he'd ever met. He could think of a dozen women who, if stranded in a storm such as this, would yell and cry and carry on like some wounded animal. Not Charity. She pitched in and did the job. That's what she'd been doing all her life and he admired her to no end for it.

Dammit, he should just walk home now. His chances of surviving the rain and lightning and gloom of the storm *had* to be better than his chances of keeping his hands off Charity MacKay if the two of them spent the night alone in his grandpappy's cabin. And the way things were adding up, that's exactly what was going to happen.

A SCATTERING OF RAINDROPS dotting Tanner's shirt, Charity watched him—efficient, muscular, macho—tie his side of the plane to a tree trunk. As a blast of wind raked the trees against the sky, pulled at her hair and bucked the plane, the rope connected to her side slid through her fingers like cooked spaghetti through a fork tine.

Tanner yelled, ''Hold on.''

Duh. That's what she was *supposed* to be doing instead of watching him. This was *not* putting her thoughts about Tanner Davenport under control as she'd planned to do while driving home from Alvena's.

Tanner ran around the plane and grabbed the rope as she snatched it from the ground. Together they pulled against another gust. He said, "Like trying to tame a wild horse."

"Try the whole blasted herd." She dug her boot heels into the ground, her back muscles aching at the strain. The plane was Tanner's pride and joy and he couldn't loose it—even though, to her, it was an instrument of torture. She knew all about losing important things, things treasured and held dear. She pulled harder.

This was better. Hey, she could work with him and not ogle his chestnut hair and fine muscles. She could spend the night with him without obsessing over his manly nature. She gave Tanner a sideways glance. *Liar, liar, pants on fire.*

Tanner nodded at an oak. "Wrap the rope around the trunk. I'll hold the plane down."

She did as instructed and in a flash he was beside her, tying some fancy knots, anchoring the plane to the tree. He faced her, grinning like a jack-o'-lantern in a rainstorm. He took off his jacket and wrapped it around her.

"Now you'll get soaked."

"We'll take turns. Thanks for helping with the plane. We did it. Though if you were fifty pounds heavier and built like Schwarzenegger this whole thing would have been a lot easier.''

"You should have stopped at *thanks.*''

He laughed and swooped her into his arms, twirling into the breeze and raindrops. Grown women didn't get picked up. Least, not usually. Least, not her.

"You are so damn beautiful, Charity MacKay. It takes my breath away.''

Her heart soared. She braced her arms on his shoulders. "Thought you wanted Schwarzenegger.''

"Couldn't tell Schwarzenegger he was beautiful and live to talk about it.'' Tanner gave her a smile that lit the world and suddenly she did feel beautiful. Then he kissed her, again, making her feel alive and special. How was she supposed to get over his kisses when he kept giving them?

Right now she didn't care. Somewhere between saving the farm, horses and MacKay pride, life had passed her by. Until this moment. Until Tanner Davenport had come along and kissed her till her toes curled.

His lips were sinfully sweet, just the right pressure, just the right tenderness, just the right…everything. He took his mouth away—hers begged for more—his eyes dark, his breath quick and hot. She wiped rain from his forehead and laughed out loud. "Why'd you kiss me?'' *Attraction? Desire? Lust?*

"Gratitude.''

G-gratitude? Gratitude! He couldn't have surprised

her more if he'd lit a firecracker and put it in her ear. "The first time you kissed me because you admire me, and this kiss is a pay-off?"

He shrugged. "You hugged me when I landed the plane. A kiss seemed appropriate."

"Sending thank-you notes is *appropriate,* Tanner. Opening a door for a woman is *appropriate.*"

"What are you getting at?"

What *was* she getting at? And why did she ask him *why* in the first place? Would she ever learn to accept things without delving into every nook and cranny? *No,* because she had this need to control every blasted thing. "Just put me down. We're getting soaked. We have to find shelter. Drowning is a distinct possibility. Where's that cabin?"

At least she didn't have to worry about Tanner having feelings for her. That was good…sort of. Mutual attraction could be tough to get over. One-sided attractions were a minor inconvenience.

He set her on the ground and said, "We're on a mountain, we won't drown. The cabin's on the other side."

"Why didn't you just land there? It would have been a shorter walk."

"It's a hill. Planes hate hills and, believe it or not, I intended to land back at the house where there wouldn't be any walk at all." Lightning flashed and the rain kicked up a notch. "Let's go before there's a barbecue and we're the main course.'' He snagged her hand. "It's slippery. Hold on to me."

She took her hand back. "No need. I'm a double for Schwarzenegger."

She followed Tanner up the hillside, getting soaked to the bone. They slid more than walked down the other side. Rain fell harder. Weeds and evergreens dripped water; rocks turned dark gray from moisture. "Thought you said the cabin was here?"

"Guess it's over the next hill…or the one after."

Her eyes widened by half. "The one after?"

"Hey, I haven't been here for a while. All the hills seem the same from the sky and I was busy landing the plane."

"How do you get around Alaska without getting lost? All that snow looks the same, too."

"Maps, instruments, gut instincts."

"Does your gut have instincts in Kentucky or just in Alaska?"

He grabbed her hand. "We'll find out."

"That's not the answer I was hoping for," she replied as she stumbled after him.

Rain fell like a curtain of beads, stinging her face and head. Thank heaven for Tanner's jacket. 'Course that meant he was getting wet all over. When they got to the top of the next rise, he pointed over a new stand of young black cherry trees. They seemed to be everywhere. He said, "Look there."

"That's an old pig house. Did you have to pick the

middle of a deluge to lose your instincts? Couldn't you get us lost on a sunny day?"

"Don't get crabby on me, MacKay."

"Remind me to apologize."

He looked down at her, water dripping from his nose and chin. He grinned. "Besides, we're not lost, just misplaced."

They slid down the next slope, her boots squishing with every step, her hair hanging like a wet mop around her face. They started up the next hill and spotted the cabin behind a stand of evergreens.

"See," Tanner said as he slapped her back, jarring her to the fillings of her teeth. "My instincts are alive and well in Kentucky."

"More like you're lucky as all get-out."

"That, too. Come on, loser builds the fire."

They raced to the cabin, splashing and sliding till they clamored up onto the porch, the floorboards clattering. Tanner shoved open the door and Charity darted inside. He slammed the door closed, then leaned back, the rain and wind howling on the other side. "Feel as if I've gone through a car wash without a car."

"I hear water dripping."

"I think it's us. Grandpappy lived here when he first bought Thistledown, though at the time Grandma called it *that dang farm.* She was kind of a city-slicker." Tanner struck a lighter.

"Where'd that come from?"

"Back pocket. In Alaska you don't leave home without a lighter."

Tanner held it high and she caught a glimpse of wooden chairs, a neat table with a bowl in the center, bunk beds made up with dry blankets.

"All the comforts of home."

"I didn't know this place was here."

"Nate keeps it up. Sentimental reasons, probably. The hands use it once in a while if they get stuck. I used to come out when…when I needed some space. Ah, the lantern's still on the mantel. Some things never change."

More thunder shook the rafters and the rain on the roof sounded like marbles being dropped from on high. Tanner lit the lantern wick and a soft, golden glow fell around him. Charity couldn't help but wonder how one man could look so virile and sexy with his hair slicked to his head as if he were some oily character in a silent movie.

She snagged some logs from the pile beside the hearth and tossed them into the fireplace. "Give me that lighter. We're both freezing."

"Grandma wasn't the only city-slicker." He handed her the lantern, then chucked paper and scraps of wood in with the logs. Setting flame to the paper, Tanner said, "In Alaska sometimes the only thing between me and the grave is a warm fire." They both watched as the wood caught, quickly turning the flames into a blaze. "We should take off our clothes."

He turned to her, surprise on his face as if he didn't quite believe what he'd said. For a second the only sounds were the crackle of fire, the storm and Charity's heart pounding like a horse's at the finish line.

"I mean—" Tanner cleared his throat "—we should wrap up in a blanket…*blankets*. Wrap ourselves in blankets. One for each," he added quickly. "Till our clothes dry. We're cold." He nodded at the bunks. "See? Blankets. You first. I'll look for food. Yeah, that's what I'll do. Food would be good here. Got to be *something* around to take our minds off…off the rain." He let out a sigh and rubbed his forehead. "It's going to be one damn long night, Charity MacKay."

"Why are you so nervous?"

He glanced back at her, taking her in. His eyes darkened.

"Are you worried about the plane?"

"No." His voice sounded thick and a little unsteady. Slowly he stepped toward her and straightened the collar of his jacket, which she wore. His fingers brushed her neck, his gaze locked with hers. Heat radiated to every part of her body and it had nothing to do with the fire in the hearth. She licked her lips, which suddenly felt dry, and she could barely breathe. Then he bent his head and kissed her.

She felt weak, then strong, as his firm, demanding

mouth molded to hers. She touched his face, feeling the slick drops of water mix with the rough texture of his five-o'clock shadow. Her fingers trailed down his long throat and around his strong neck. He kissed the corner of her mouth then her neck and behind her left ear. Shivers danced up her spine and desire lodged in her belly. His arms slid around her back, bringing her body to him, his arousal pressing into her middle.

Holy moley. Neck, arms, chest were part of the kissing thing. But the part of his anatomy pressing against her at the moment went beyond kissing.

He pulled back and she hated it. Being in Tanner's arms and kissing and knowing what effect she had on him, and what effect he had on her, seemed incredible. She didn't want it to end. She gazed at him, her heart pounding. "I'm not exactly the diva of kissing, but that was no gratitude kiss."

"It was a mistake kiss."

"We've gone from gratitude to mistake. This isn't progress."

Rainwater dripped from his chin and clumped his lashes together with moisture. He pulled in a ragged breath and stepped away from her, the light of the fire casting dark shadows on his face. "In ten days I'm out of here and…and I'm not into one-night stands. Or even ten-day stands, for that matter, least not with you. There can't be any *progress* between us. There can't be anything between us." He looked at her. "Right?"

He massaged the back of his neck. She'd rather have him massage the back of *her* neck or any place else he wanted to massage. But that wouldn't happen, for all the reasons Tanner had given her. "How about maybe?"

"Maybe? I'm not staying and you're not going, and you're not the casual-sex type. No maybe."

She gave him a woman-of-the-world look. Least, that's what she hoped it was. "How do you know? I'm very wordly."

"When you say something, you mean it. When you give something—" his eyes turned mahogany "—you commit to it forever. Your world is here, and that world doesn't work for me. My father wanted me to raise horses like he did and when I didn't he kicked me out—out of his life, out of the family and out of his will. As if I didn't exist. When I'm here, no matter how welcome Nate makes me feel, that's all I remember. Not belonging. But you belong here as much as every tree and horse and house. There is no 'maybe' for us."

He shook his head as if suddenly very tired of the whole idea. "We should eat. Think I'll go outside and catch us a bear."

"You might find a can of something lurking around."

"That would work." He crossed the room. "You

better change.'' He tossed her a towel from a shelf. ''Use two blankets. Two blankets would be good. It's…cold.''

She watched him carefully place logs on the fire, as if doing one thing and thinking of something else. She peeled off her blouse and jeans to hang by the fire to dry. She'd keep her bra and panties on. There could be nothing between her and Tanner. But she couldn't be buck-naked around him no matter how many excuses he had for not getting involved. Not that *she* didn't agree with every word he'd said, but her hormones sure didn't. They didn't get it at all. They were near red alert no matter how she tried to tell them they were red-alerting for nothing.

TANNER LOOKED AROUND the cabin, at any place but Charity. Food. There must be food somewhere. He needed something to take his mind off kissing her and wanting to make love to her. He wanted both so much, his teeth ached. 'Course another part of his anatomy ached a lot more, but he wasn't going to think about that. The thought of Charity wrapped in a blanket was enticing as hell no matter how much he tried to convince himself this was a wrong-guy-for-the-wrong-girl scenario. ''Chili or soup?''

''Huh?'' she asked from across the dimly lit room.

Firelight danced on the wood floor and over the plank ceilings. The scent of burning hickory hung in the cabin. It was warmer now. He thought of Charity.

Too warm. "There are cans and an opener and some plates and a jug over here."

"I vote chili."

She came up beside him, draped in a blanket, her hair fanned out to dry, and she looked all soft and warm and cuddly. She surveyed his find, then picked up the gray jug sitting beside the canned goods. "Looks like Deryl Pruit's moonshine." She pointed to the red-painted X on the front, then pulled out the cork with a hollow pop. Her blanket gaped in front. Whatever that jug contained couldn't be as distracting as that exposed soft skin.

Charity sniffed the contents of the jug and her eyes watered. "Yep, that's Deryl's. After a couple drinks of this stuff we won't have to worry about any *maybes* between us. We'll be too zonked to care about anything."

"You really intend to drink that shine?"

She splashed a portion into two tin cups, picked one up and saluted Tanner. "To impossible relationships."

She gulped. Her eyes watered more and her mouth parted in a perfect *O*. How he wanted to kiss that *O*.

She coughed and sputtered. *"Wow!"*

Yeah, that's exactly how he felt about her. But he shouldn't. He grabbed his cup and took a sip, letting it burn a path down his throat. He concentrated on the burn and not the woman next to him. "We need a pot to hang over the fire."

"You change, then set the table. I'll cook. Too bad we don't have *my* pie."

He swallowed another mouthful. Had the top of his head just separated from the bottom? Good. That would keep his mind off Charity. After sipping this stuff, he wouldn't have a mind. It would evaporate thanks to the alcohol. "Check the pockets of my jacket."

"You put my pie in your pocket?"

"Not exactly." He crossed to the beds and tossed her his jacket, which she'd left there. With her back to him as she searched the pockets, he peeled off his shirt and jeans. He wrapped himself in a blanket that covered him to his knees. He might be turned on as all get-out but there was no chance of Charity returning the sentiment. Nate hadn't called him Old Chicken Legs for nothing.

"Well, I'll be darned," Charity said as she held up the jacket. "Amazing what you find in pockets these days. Army knife, squashed KitKat, and maybe we can use this rock here to flavor the chili."

She flipped it to him and he caught it midair as she asked, "Alaskan lucky piece?"

He looked at it for a long moment. "Kentucky memorabilia. From the creek that runs through Thistledown." He went to the table and took another drink of liquid fire from the tin cup. "Nate and I used to send our stick boats down. I'd make up stories about where they landed. As long as I put horses in the story, he'd listen.''

''I did that with Savannah, but the story always had to end with shopping at Bloomingdale's.''

Tanner rubbed his thumb over the rock's edges, smoothed by this very motion. ''Don't know why I keep this thing around. Reminds me of Nate, I guess.''

Charity stirred the pot over the fire. ''I'd go berserk if I moved away from the farm and Savannah, Patience and Mama. I wouldn't know how to live anyplace else.''

The red, gold and auburn strands of her hair glimmered in the flickering light. ''And I wouldn't know how to live if I stayed here.''

She turned toward him and nodded, and he felt himself do the same. Like some unspoken truce that she understood their lives led them in different directions. He took in her soft lips and green eyes. Dang if they weren't like sticker bushes on his well-plotted path.

She went back to stirring; he took another drink of shine. ''Next time I flip a switch and something electrical happens,'' she said, ''I'm going to appreciate it. Think I'll enclose a thank-you note with my next electric bill.''

She snagged a cloth and took the pot from the fire, then scooped chili into the dishes.

She looked delicious and tempting—much too

tempting. He needed some other distraction than moonshine, which was tough in a one-room cabin.

"Let's talk about the wedding," he suggested. That should keep his mind off Charity wrapped in a blanket—too bad she wasn't wrapped in cellophane. Gads, the shine was rotting his brain. *Wedding, think wedding.* He sat, took a spoon, only looked halfway up so as not to connect with Charity's lovely face across the table; instead, he connected with the gaping blanket again, and this time the gape revealed nicely rounded cleavage.

He looked back at his chili. Beans were a damn sorry substitute for cleavage. "What ideas did you have for breaking up Savannah and Nate?"

Her eyes glazed over and her head wobbled as if not attached. "You've been at this longer than me. What do you think we should do? Hmm?" She gave him a lopsided smile.

He took a bite of chili. "There's still the flying idea. And now there are sick horses at Thistledown. Nate's involvement with them will show Savannah she'll always take second place to a horse. Can't imagine her putting up with that."

Charity waggled her empty cup at him. "What if we got Mary Lou Hodges to make a play for Nate. She's always liked him." Charity hiccuped. "That might work. She's more sedate than Savannah ever thought about being. More settled. It would be a good match."

"Mary Lou likes Nate because he donated money for a new wing to her library. She has gray hair, a pointed chin and the personality of the Wicked Witch of the West. All Mary Lou will do is make Nate think Savannah is the prize of the ages and want to marry her all the more. You're not very good at this sabotaging thing."

Charity put her cup down on the paint-chipped table, pushed away the chili and stacked her left hand over her right in front of her. She rested her chin on top and her eyes crossed then closed. "Boy, I'm really tired. Can't sleep. Don't have my favorite jammies."

He pictured Charity in soft pink cotton, warm, cuddly, tempting as hell. *"You…you want to sleep?"* He eyed the bunks, picturing her in one and him in the other. And he was supposed to *stay* in the other. The shine wasn't working worth a damn. That, or his desire for Charity was stronger than any booze could be. "We can't sleep. We have to come up with more ideas to break up the wedding. Lots more."

He looked back at her. Her eyes still closed, her breathing slow; she was dead asleep, sitting at the table with her chin on her hands. Okay, this worked. She was there, he was here. A table between them. He thought of her jammies, wondering what they really looked like. Forget it. He'd only want to strip them off. *Dang.*

He put the pot and dishes into the sink, pumped

water then washed and dried them. He tossed another log on the fire, kicked back in his chair and propped his feet on the hearth. He looked at Charity again. She was so incredibly beautiful, inside and out. Her breathing was easy, her lips parted, her skin glowing in the firelight. At least she would sleep tonight, but he sure wouldn't. Being in the same room as Charity and not having her in his arms was frustrating as hell.

Chapter Six

Charity awoke to the sound of someone banging on the wood-plank door—or was that banging in her head?—and sunlight streaming in through the window. Her mouth tasted like used cat litter, her eyes felt as gritty as buckshot from a twelve-gauge and her back was arched in a permanent *C*.

Alvena Cahill yelled from the other side, "Charity? Tanner? You in there?"

Charity's eyes crossed as she muttered, "The woman has a voice like a gravel pit."

More banging. "Bet something good's going on in there. I'm really sorry to put an end to it, but I had to come find you two. It's important."

Charity stood, wobbled, wrapped her blanket around her against the morning chill and swallowed a string of curses as her backbone straightened out. She looked at Tanner sitting on the chair. He pried open an eye and said, "What was in that stuff we drank last night?"

"Lava." Charity hobbled to the door, yanked it open, squinted against the sun as the shafts of light pierced holes in her skull. If she ever drank shine again she would jump off a bridge…it would be way less painful.

Alvena laughed. "You look like hell." She strode inside and peered at Tanner. "You look worse." She homed in on the jug. "Well, no wonder. Surprised you're both not dead. This stuff can kill you."

Tanner retreated into his blanket. "Guess that red X was a warning label."

Alvena went to the bunk beds and slapped the top one, sending dust motes into the air. "Still made up. Can't believe the only thing you used these beds for was the blankets. You wasted a perfect opportunity for a little hanky-panky, you know."

Charity leaned against the wall for support, her legs turning to rubber. "Tanner and I are…neighbors. No hanky or panky at either address. We just got caught in a storm together. How'd you find us?"

"Miller brothers were out checking fence and spotted the tire tracks in the mud, then saw the plane and my truck. They gave me a call and I told them about you and Tanner here. This cabin is the only shelter for a spell and since we didn't see any vultures circling this morning we figured there weren't any dead bodies and you made it here. I called your mama and said you were all right."

Charity straightened her spine against the wall, listening to it crack into place. "You were wrong about the dead part."

"Honey, that's just you doing some wishful thinking. Shine hangovers are the worst."

"Can't believe I fell asleep at the table."

Alvena shook her head. "Neither can I, nor will anybody else on the Ridge." She turned to Tanner. "What happened to you when you went to Alaska? Your brain get frozen over? I doubt if you ever slept in a chair with a pretty woman in the same room when you lived on the Ridge. Charity may be a little long in the tooth, least for you. But she's cute enough, you got to give her that."

Charity would have rolled her eyes, but it hurt too much. "Thanks for the vote of confidence."

Tanner stood and Alvena said, "Well, will you look at those legs. My donkey has better-looking legs."

He took Alvena's arm. "That's it. It's been a long, long, long night." He propelled her toward the door. "Wait outside. We'll be with you in a minute."

"Get a move on. There's a meeting at Thistledown at noon about all the ailing horses and what to do about them, and Charity needs to be in on it."

Charity's eyes widened by half and she pushed herself from the wall. "Are more horses sick?"

"Tanglewood and Homestead have two off their feed and looking poorly. None down yet, but Nate's called in people from the university."

"I'll be ready in a minute," Charity replied.

"I'm going to work on the plane, see if I can get her going," Tanner explained.

Alvena opened the door. "Time's a'wastin'."

She closed the door behind her and Charity hitched her chin in that direction. "I think that's Kentucky's version of the CIA."

Tanner came to her and cupped her chin in his palm, tipping her face to his. Morning stubble darkened his jaw and his hair fell over his forehead. His blanket rode low on his shoulders, revealing the soft curly chest hair that had driven her nuts the day before. Nothing had changed.

"Smile," he said.

"The nuclear explosions going off in my head forbid it."

"Humor me."

She did as he asked and he said, "Just as I thought, no long teeth." He kissed her forehead. "Thanks for helping with the plane. I owe you."

"Oh, I'll think of something." Did she have to make it sound so provocative and sexy even though there could be nothing between them?

Yes. She couldn't help it. After all, she was a woman and he was a breath away, looking handsome as hell—chicken legs, stubble and all. There was a spark in Tanner's eyes that hadn't been there a second ago…

Alvena yelled, "Jiminy Cricket, you going to take

all day or are you catching up on unfinished business?''

They had unfinished business, all right, but it was going to stay that way. The spark was still in Tanner's eyes, but he only said, ''You better change.''

''I kind of liked the blanket look.''

He arched his left eyebrow and tweaked her nose. ''It had its merits. But you and I in blankets is more temptation than I want to think about now.''

He turned around and she studied his back for a moment, feeling temptation singe a path right through her. Nine more days till the wedding. How would she stay away from Tanner for nine more days? ''Maybe we should have given in to that temptation last night?''

Slowly he turned back to her, his eyes smoky. ''All we'd do is start something we can't finish and there's too much between us for a brief fling in the sheets.''

She bit her lip. ''A fling sounds pretty good to me.''

He grinned, but his eyes turned to dark chocolate. ''Then what? When I fly in once in a while to see Nate, we pick up where we left off?''

Another bang on the door followed by, ''Yoo-hoo. Anybody alive in there? We need to get to that meeting.''

Tanner went to the hearth and snatched Charity's clothes. ''Get dressed. You have horses to tend to and I have a plane that needs attention.''

She took the clothes and he turned his back to her. "You can take care of your plane later. Come with me to support Nathan."

"Thistledown isn't mine. I don't belong there, never have, never will. Nathan can handle it."

Dressed, she made for the door, then paused with her hand on the knob. He was so sexy and so off limits and so much a hardhead. "I understand about you and me not getting involved, but not this. You flew all the way in from Alaska to watch out for Nathan, but as soon as Thistledown enters the picture you back off. You're better than that, Tanner."

"I have no good feelings about the farm and don't care what happens to it. That's Nate's business, not mine. I'm not getting involved with Thistledown no matter how much you want me to." His eyes hardened, his jaw clenched. "Fact is, I was pretty much told to stay the hell away from it and not come back."

"Not by Nathan. Put the past where it belongs."

"Easy for the oldest sister of the Brady Bunch to say."

"Who needs a dunking in the water trough now, Tanner Davenport?"

AND TWO HOURS LATER as she and Mama drove up the winding lane to the main house at Thistledown, she wanted to dunk Tanner in the trough more than ever. Tyrannical father or not, Tanner should be there for his brother. Times were tough and that's when families pulled together. That much she knew from experience.

She parked the station wagon and got out as Mama said, "Everyone in the county's here."

Not everyone, Charity thought. As they walked toward the house, Mama nodded to Nathan standing at the doorway, greeting his guests. "He looks awful. I wonder where Savannah is. Doc gave her the day off, and she needs to be here with her intended at a time like this."

Charity fell into step. "She's getting refreshments together for the guests."

Mama stopped dead in the middle of the brick sidewalk. "Savannah? *Our* Savannah, who can't boil water, is going to cook for guests?" She took Charity's hand. "We have to stop her right now before we all wind up in the hospital. Who will care for the horses then? Think of the lawsuits. Oh, my stars. Remember the Christmas cookies last year and how the gun club used them for skeet?"

Charity bit back a laugh. "Nathan's housekeeper is doing the preparation. Savannah's helping with setting it up and serving."

"Well, I'll be. The age of miracles is not dead. Savannah MacKay, the little homemaker."

"More like Savannah in love with Nathan and wanting to help even though she doesn't know anything about the horse business." And a little nudging from older sister who didn't want Tanner's plan about Savannah not being part of Nathan's life to come true.

Charity's idea of pretending to help Tanner so that she could find out how he intended to stop the wedding had so far worked out perfectly. Sort of *perfectly*.

Spending time with him was…tedious. She didn't want to like him. She really, really didn't. But that's not the way things had worked out…except for now when he wasn't there. Great brown eyes and hair and a body that wouldn't quit were nice attributes but didn't compensate for a lack of consideration. Heck, maybe he wasn't such a terrific guy, after all. Maybe she had him all wrong. Now if she could just get her hormones to believe that.

As she and Mama entered the Georgian, the brass chandelier in the hallway glimmered in the noon sunlight. They followed the others into the living room where the doors had been pushed back to accommodate everyone.

The owners of Ivy Creek, Green Gate, Tall Oaks and other multimillion-dollar Thoroughbred farms sat in the living room. She knew them all. Everybody knew everybody in this business and they were all in trouble, big and little farms alike.

Charity found seats for her and Mama. They smiled at Savannah as she passed around antique sterling silver cups of punch and cut-glass tumblers of the finest Kentucky bourbon. The cups remained on the tray: this was a bourbon situation. Mama nodded to Nathan

NO POSTAGE
NECESSARY
IF MAILED
IN THE
UNITED STATES

BUSINESS REPLY MAIL

FIRST-CLASS MAIL   PERMIT NO. 717-003   BUFFALO, NY

POSTAGE WILL BE PAID BY ADDRESSEE

HARLEQUIN READER SERVICE
3010 WALDEN AVE
PO BOX 1867
BUFFALO NY 14240-9952

Get FREE BOOKS and a FREE GIFT when you play the...

LAS VEGAS
GAME

Just scratch off the gold box with a coin. Then check below to see the gifts you get!

YES!
I have scratched off the gold Box. Please send me my **2 FREE BOOKS** and **gift for which I qualify.** I understand that I am under no obligation to purchase any books as explained on the back of this card.

354 HDL DVEN   154 HDL DVE4

FIRST NAME	LAST NAME

ADDRESS

APT.#	CITY

STATE/PROV.	ZIP/POSTAL CODE

(H-AR-02/04)

7	7	7	Worth TWO FREE BOOKS plus a BONUS Mystery Gift!
🍒	🍒	🍒	Worth TWO FREE BOOKS!
🔔	🔔	☘	TRY AGAIN!

Visit us online at
www.eHarlequin.com

Offer limited to one per household and not valid to current Harlequin American Romance® subscribers. All orders subject to approval.

as he took his place by the hearth. "He looks bushed. Do you mind if I stay here for a bit and see if I can help him out? Our place isn't as hard hit as Thistledown. I wonder where Tanner is."

Charity groused more to herself than Mama. "The Red Barron is preoccupied."

She studied Nathan, tired, drained, worried. *Blast Tanner Davenport.* He had some nerve to suggest that Savannah wouldn't understand Nathan during this crisis and then not be here himself.

"Friends," greeted Nathan, "thank you for coming. We have a serious problem. It's not only a business problem but the lives of our horses and this year's foals are at stake, and it's our responsibility to protect them. More than money, more than racing, more than winning, what keeps us in this business is our love of horses."

He nodded to the men and women standing beside him. "These veterinarians from the university and the Department of Agriculture are here to help us find answers. The only thing that seems different this spring from other springs is the unusual dryness. What that has to do with our horses getting sick is what we have to figure out. Or maybe it's not that at all. Maybe some chemical has leached its way into our water supply."

For an hour Charity listened intently to the discussion until Alvena Cahill stood up and said, "The one item that seems to offer relief to the sick horses around here is Margaret MacKay's yeast concoction.'' She pointed at the vets. ''I suggest you take her back to that university of yours and make enough of her remedy for all of us till we find some answers.''

Mama blushed as the vets folded their arms and offered patronizing smiles. They assured everyone the problems with the horses went beyond mountain remedies and folklore. Modern science would find a way to help them out of this situation.

The crowd nodded and Mama's blush deepened. Charity took her hand. Mama didn't need more public embarrassment. With a no-good gambling husband and a bankrupt farm, she'd had her fill of it over the years. *Darn it!* Mama's remedy worked. Charity stood, thinking how best to tell the pompous asses from the university and everyone else in the room that they had pea brains and—

Her words died in her throat as Tanner sauntered into the room, grubby and muddy as a hound dog on the hunt. Her jaw hit the floor. Least, that's the way it felt. Tanner *did* show up and, judging from his appearance, he'd walked from the cabin to get here. He was barefoot, probably left his boots outside in deference to the Orientals covering the floors.

He rested his hand on Nathan's shoulder, said something that made his brother laugh, then turned to the group. ''I don't know much about horses, but the Eskimos have a herb that treats hypothermia and saved my butt last year when I got caught in an ice storm. The point being, if something works, even a folk remedy, use it."

Charity plopped back down onto the Chippendale chair as Tanner continued. "We all know Margaret MacKay has been curing folks and animals for years on the Ridge. Bet there's not one of you who hasn't asked her advice one time or another over the years. If she has something to keep your horses going till the good doctors find a cure for what ails them, why not listen to her?"

Nods and murmurs of agreement slowly filled the room and Charity felt a knot the size of Kentucky lodge in her throat. Not only had Tanner come to stand beside his brother in the house he despised, he'd defended Mama.

His gaze met Charity's and he gave her a what-the-hell-am-I-doing-here look. She grinned and winked, knowing very well what he was doing here and admiring him so much for it. Brown eyes, muscles, dented chin were really nice, but they didn't hold a candle to loyalty and kindness.

When the meeting broke up, a few of the horse owners came over to Mama, wanting to know about her remedy for the sick horses. Pride welled up inside Charity. Mama was wonderful, talented and smart. And now, thanks to Tanner, everyone realized this, including Mama.

Charity approached Tanner as he talked to Nathan. "Where's your plane? Didn't hear you land."

"Plane's parked where we left it. Clogged fuel pump. I must be losing my touch, and I don't want to hear about horses not getting clogged fuel pumps."

"Wouldn't think of it."

His lips pulled into a slow smile. "You're not going to let me forget this, are you?"

Nathan grinned. "Heard you two spent the night at the cabin. Bet that was interesting."

Tanner shrugged. "Got caught in the storm."

Nathan's grin grew. "Savannah and I used that excuse once or twice."

He slapped Tanner on the back. "Thanks for helping out. Now I'd better go massage the egos of our guests from the university. Right now they're not nearly as popular as Mama Kay and we do need them to get this problem under control."

Nathan strode off and Charity looked back at Tanner. "Didn't expect to see you here."

"Neither did I." He raked his hair. "Amazing how a dunking in the water trough can bring you to your senses." He tweaked her nose. "You were right, least about helping Nate. I don't have any good feelings about Thistledown and still don't feel I belong, but Nate's my family." He nodded toward the door. "Let's go outside, this house makes me crazy."

"But you came."

He studied her for a moment, his eyes dark and mysterious. "Yeah, Kentucky Girl, I came."

They turned for the door but Mama cut them off.

Her blue eyes wide and smiling as if her horse had won the Derby. "You'll never guess what just happened. The man from the Department of Agriculture asked me to come to Lexington to talk to him and his associates about my remedies for the sick horses."

Had Mama ever been this excited in her life? If so, Charity hadn't witnessed it. Mama continued, "They're actually interested in what I have to say."

Charity swallowed a groan. She didn't want to rain on Mama's parade, but she hated to see her go and suffer at the hands of the know-it-all vets who had put her down earlier.

"That's wonderful, Mama." Charity smiled. "Puck should go with you." Puck would clobber anyone who hurt Mama. "The wagon's not safe for that distance and…and you won't get lonely, and you'll have fun together in Lexington and—"

Mama giggled. Her mother actually *giggled?* "That's just what I thought. I'll ask him as soon as we get home."

Mama's grin dropped a notch. "But who will help you with the horses? And the wedding. What about all the final preparations for that?"

"Everything's almost done. Savannah can handle the rest and Patience can help her."

Mama took Tanner's hand. "Tanner will help you if you need anything. He sure came through for me today." She stood on tiptoes and kissed him on the cheek. "Thank you, dear. I'm so glad you're here."

Red inched up Tanner's neck and he swallowed. "Don't think anyone ever said that to me in this room before." He laughed, but it didn't sound like a happy laugh.

Charity put her arm around Mama. "Go. Show those hotshots a thing or two."

Mama looked at Charity then Tanner. "You really think I *should* go?"

Tanner chuckled. "I sure do. If Charity has a problem, you and Puck will only be a couple of hours away."

"Then I'll do it. Puck and I will need to leave tonight."

Everything would be okay. Puck would make sure of that. Savannah had Nathan, Mama had Puck. Charity realized she never had any man to care about her like that. Tanner was the closest, he *had* given her his jacket. Her life was pathetic.

Tanner watched Mama join the vets, then took Charity's arm and propelled her out the doorway, down the steps and onto the sidewalk. She looked at him. "Do you want me to give you a lift back to the plane? Mama might be here awhile making arrangements."

"What's Savannah doing here?" He hitched his chin at the house.

"Serving refreshments?"

He folded his arms. "I thought the plan was to keep

her *away* from Nate, not help him. She was supposed to realize he didn't have time for her, remember?''

Charity put her left hand on her hip, her very shapely hip, and pursed her lips, her very kissable lips, then said, ''Perhaps you want me to lock Savannah in her room and swallow the key.''

''If that's what it takes.''

Tanner looked back at the doorway. How could he be in this state of arousal—again? Because just thinking about Charity's lips and hips, after spending the night with her in a gaping blanket, would be enough to drive any man over the edge. Hell, at this point he could get excited over a toenail if it belonged to her. Now that he thought about it, she *did* have cute toenails. Hot-pink.

Damnation. Every muscle in his body—especially the muscles right below his belt—were as hard as baked brick. He looked at Nate and Savannah standing in the doorway of the house as Charity said, ''They sure look like the happiest couple on the Ridge.''

Tanner shook his head to clear his mind and caught a whiff of…Charity. He'd know that scent anywhere, better than magnolias or fresh rain or fried chicken. He had a sudden lust attack, and not for chicken. ''What couple?''

''Savannah? Nathan? At the front door talking to friends? I think that moonshine corroded your brain.

The two of them look content. Maybe it's a sign that they *do* belong together.''

''No way.'' He collected his thoughts about the wedding and kicked out the ones about Charity. At least, he tried to. ''Okay, Savannah helped this time, but she needs to realize the horses will always come first with Nate. Can you think of *anything* she needs him for? You know, some last-minute plans or the guest list or anything at all?''

''Tonight one of Savannah's friends is throwing them a couples' shower.''

''That's perfect. Nate will be too busy with the horses tonight to go anywhere, and Savannah'll want him to go to the shower. She'll throw one of her hissy fits, the kind she has when things don't go her way. Then Nate will be upset that she's upset. I'll point out to him this is the way it's always going to be— Savannah being demanding. You point out to Savannah that she'll always take second place to the horses.'' He looked at Charity. ''Why are you shaking your head? Better for them to find out now this is the way life will be once they're married. Right?''

''Savannah's changed, she won't throw a fit. Nate's changed. The world doesn't revolve around his business twenty-four/seven. He realizes there's room for something else, like a life, like love.''

This time Tanner shook his head and looked at her, hair dancing in the breeze, skin fresh as the springtime around them. ''Care to make a little wager on how this plays out?''

Her eyes darkened a shade, desire sparked deep inside. ''Wager? What?''

Damn, he was going to bet the pie. But after a look like that, to hell with pie, a night in her arms seemed a great wager. Oh, what he wouldn't give to win *that* wager. But, no, a night with Charity would only be a one-night stand and that was a bad idea. There'd be too much entanglement, too much emotion, too much to walk away from, and everybody would get hurt when he left. They'd already had this discussion, and that's why they'd spent the night sleeping in chairs. ''Pie.''

Her eyes shot wide open. *''Pie?''*

''Alvena Cahill's.''

''Pie?''

''You ate it, didn't you? I knew it.''

''It's at the house, in its entirety. Some of us, unlike others—'' she arched her brow in his direction ''—have willpower.''

''I have willpower, just not when it comes to pie.'' He watched her smile, could almost feel her in his arms. His willpower waned and it wasn't for pie.

''Then it's settled,'' he continued. He held out his hand and she took it. Not a swift move on his part. Touching Charity made his head swim and his heart race. If he felt this way now, what would happen if he kissed her again?

No kissing, just pie.

He dropped her hand as if it were a hot coal. "Pie it is."

FOUR HOURS LATER, after he'd retrieved the biplane, he walked to the stable, looking for Nate and still thinking about that pie. Actually, he was still thinking about Charity, but if he could lie to himself often enough maybe he'd begin to believe this fabrication.

He found Nate mixing feed for the horses, but before he could say anything, the phone rang and Nate picked it up.

At first Nate's face brightened. However, after a few minutes and no talking on his part, Nate hung up, his brow furrowed.

"What's wrong? More horses sick?"

Nate sighed. "It was Savannah. We were *supposed* to go to a shower tonight. She reminded me earlier, but with all the commotion around here and the horses…" He waved his hand across the feed. "I forgot."

Yes! This was it. "Was Savannah mad?"

Nate stroked his chin. "Said she'd come over later. Said we needed to talk."

Well, hot damn! Needing to talk was always bad news for a relationship—or in this case, good news. These kinds of talks usually went something like, "We can still be friends, *but*…" or "You'll always be special to me *but*...'' But always came in there somewhere and right now that's what mattered.

Tanner put his hand on Nate's shoulder. "Everything's going to be fine. It may be a little rocky for a while but things will straighten out."

He hated seeing his brother so miserable, but it was for the best. He and Savannah were as different as peas and apples. Tanner nodded at the barrel of feed. "Want me to help you out here? If you mix it, I'll give it to the horses."

"I told the boys to take a couple hours off. Everyone's been working like mad. If you could give me a hand, that would really help." He passed Tanner a bucket of some concoction. "Add this to what's in the stalls. Mama Kay said it keeps toxins from being ingested. Watch out for Buckshot and Tinsel. They're cantankerous, especially around strangers."

Tanner grinned. "And I bet they're fast as greased lightning."

Nate's exhausted features pulled into a grin. "Faster." He wiped the back of his hand across his wrinkled brow. "Thanks for pitching in. I know working around horses isn't your thing."

"If you need help, I'll help. Just say the word." Tanner took the bucket from Nate, left the feed room and started his rounds of the stalls. The sound of his boots on concrete mixed with the soft nicker of the horses. He'd almost forgotten the smells of fresh hay and oats in these barns and he waited for the distaste for it all to well up inside him as it always had. But it didn't.

He stopped scooping the mixture into Buckshot's feed and gently stroked the stallion. Maybe he felt the way he did because this time he wanted to be here. Somehow that made all the difference.

"Hey, Tanner," came Nate's voice from outside the stall.

Tanner gave Buckshot one last pat and closed the half door to the stall behind him. Nate handed him a cell phone. "Savannah's here." He pulled in a deep breath. "I'll only be gone about twenty minutes or so. Do you mind holding the fort? I really, really need to…talk to her now. The rest of the staff isn't due back for fifteen minutes or so and I don't like to leave the horses when I don't know what's going on around here. I could wait till the others get back, but I don't want to." He nodded at the phone. "If you have a problem, hit three on speed dial."

"Your private line?"

"Barn manager. He's having dinner, but if you need him he'll be here in a flash."

Nate raked his hair and Tanner said, "It'll be okay. Savannah isn't the only woman in the world, if she wants to break up over a silly shower and—"

"Break up?" Nate's eyes widened by half.

Tanner put his hand on Nate's shoulder and gave him a sympathetic look. "She's not here to discuss the weather. She's pissed as hell you missed the shower. She doesn't understand that you have work to do and these horses are your life.''

Nate put his hand on Tanner's shoulder and a sly smile crept across his face. ''Actually, Savannah's in my room taking a bubble bath. Something about a fragrance called Ravish.''

Nate reddened, his tired eyes danced, he licked his lips and stretched his arms out in front of him, hands clasped in reverse, cracking his knuckles in a ready-for-action gesture. ''She wants me to come join her.''

''You're kidding,''

Nate grinned like a tomcat on the prowl. ''Do I look like a man who's kidding?''

Tanner watched Nate head for the main door of the stable, not quite believing what he saw. Nate Davenport was leaving his horses for a bubble bath. A bubble bath in Ravish! He thought of Charity and the perfume store and Ravish and how he'd nearly taken her right there in the front display window and made passionate love to her in front of Savannah and the salesladies and the whole damn population of Bluegrass Ridge, Kentucky. *Dang,* he should have told Nate that twenty minutes wasn't near long enough.

Tanner looked around the stable. Something seemed wrong with this picture. *He* was feeding horses while his brother was having a bubble bath with his intended. And to top it off, Tanner now got to tell Charity MacKay she was right, Savannah didn't have a hissy. 'Course he'd need to wait till

Nate came back from his Ravishing bubble bath to tell Charity that.

He thought of her and the perfume on her wrists. His insides burned like Hades, and that's exactly where he'd be if he started anything with her. They'd get more involved and it couldn't go anywhere.

But he really liked her…her flame-red hair, her green eyes, her sexy shape and her determination and tenacity. How could he *not* like her? But he could do nothing about it…except eat pie.

Chapter Seven

Charity eyed Mama's four-poster bed covered with old, out-of-style clothes and Charity exchanged looks with Patience, who sat on the far end of the bed. Together they watched Mama fold a ten-year-old sweater into a twenty-year-old suitcase.

Patience asked, "When are you and Puck going to Lexington? The vets just talked to you this afternoon, they can't expect you before tomorrow."

"We're going to take off as soon as we get packed, dear. We need to do something as quickly as possible. If we get there by tonight, we can start in the morning. You'll help Charity while we're gone, won't you?"

A faded skirt followed the sweater and Patience bit back a frown. "You should go shopping in Lexington, Mama. Get some new things."

Charity added, "We can afford it."

Mama shrugged. "Nonsense. My clothes are fine and dandy. I just add that string of your grandmother's pearls to anything I put on and it looks wonderful.'' Mama picked up a pair of black heels, the scuffs touched up with magic marker. ''Maybe I should put these in a bag first. Don't want to get my nice things dirty.'' She laughed. ''I hate to pack for a trip. Always have. Now I think I forget how, been so long and all.''

Patience stood and took the shoes. ''You should see how Puck's doing, and Charity and I will take care of your packing. It's already after six. You don't want to be driving through the hills in the dark.''

Mama smiled. ''You know, the university is putting us up in a fancy hotel.''

Charity took Mama's hand. ''That's the least they can do for you. You have all the answers. They need you. They should treat you like a queen.''

Patience kissed Mama's cheek. ''We're so proud of you, we could pop.''

Mama giggled. ''Me, too. And I'm so excited.''

She scurried from the bedroom like a teenager on her first date, and Patience turned to Charity, pointed to the bed and groaned. ''Whatever are we going to do about this? We can't let Mama go to Lexington looking *vintage*.''

''Grab some towels from the linen closet.''

Patience's eyes widened. ''You want Mama to wear towels? Have you lost your mind? You've been spending too much time with those horses. Your brain has gone to seed.''

She leveled Patience with a steely look, the kind granted big sisters from birth.

Patience threw her hands in the air. "Everybody's always ordering me around. Think they can tell me what to do because I'm the youngest and—"

"We don't have a whole lot of time for the woe-is-me game, Patience. Just get the darn towels, will you?"

Charity went into her own bedroom and pulled the credit card from the checkbook. The card was for business and emergencies. She thought of Mama's clothes. *Emergency.* Charity went back into Mama's room, grabbed a nightgown and toothbrush, took out the old sweater and skirt and said to Patience, "Put the towels in the suitcase."

"You're nuts."

Charity dropped the nightgown and toothbrush on top of the towels, then the credit card on top of that. "Now Mama will have to shop."

She shut the suitcase and Patience stared at it a moment and grinned. "She'll think she has clothes and she won't. I take it back, you're brilliant."

"Now if I could only have that in writing."

"Dream on, sister dear. Such declarations are only made in private with no witnesses or tape recorders." She snatched up the suitcase and Charity followed her down the stairs and out the front door to the station wagon. Puck put the suitcase next to his in the back and got in the driver's side, next to Mama. He poked his head out the open window. "Call if you need help."

He and Mama waved as they took off down the drive, then Charity said, "Hope Mama and Puck find time to have a little fun in Lexington. They deserve it." She yawned. "I'm going to spend the night with the horses, I'm beat."

Patience laughed. "Guess last night wore you out, huh. Heard you and Tanner spent the night in his granddaddy's cabin." She winked.

Charity folded her arms and retrieved her big-sister look from before. "We got caught in a storm. Period. Nothing more."

"Well, if that's the truth—which I sincerely hope it isn't—you aren't nearly as brilliant as I said. In case you haven't noticed, men like Tanner Davenport don't come around every day, especially on the Ridge."

Charity stared at Patience as she headed toward the back door. All day she'd told herself she'd done the right thing by staying out of Tanner's arms, away from his kisses and out of his bed. They'd agreed on a noninvolvement policy.

Well, guess what? She was already involved, at least the lusty side of her was. She wanted Tanner right now, naked in her arms, and she'd work out the details later. Except not even the UN could work out *these* details. It couldn't move Alaska to Kentucky, make her love flying and adventure, make him love horses and horse farms and help both of them be on the same side, to make this marriage between Nathan and Savannah go through without a hitch.

And that brought up another wrinkle. If Tanner ever found out how she'd been working against him to stop the wedding when she was supposed to be his partner, he'd have her guilty hide made into slipcovers for his plane. This was not the stuff relationships were built on.

Now that she'd straightened herself out, she'd spend the rest of the night in peace, away from Tanner and with her horses. She checked Silver Bell, who still wasn't eating much, but she *was* eating something. That was more than could be said about some of the other sick horses on the Ridge. Charity checked on Misty Kay, then took a blanket from a chest, where she stored extras along with a pillow and a few books. This wasn't the first night she'd kept watch over horses. It wouldn't be the last.

She pushed two bales of hay together against the wall, then spread the blanket. She sat with her knees drawn to her chest, chin perched on top, gazing out the double open barn doors.

Splashes of red, pink, blue and purple topped the hills in a blaze of glory as the sun sank to the horizon. The earth seemed to stand still as it always did at this time, as if it needed a rest from the problems of the day. How often had she witnessed sunsets from this doorway? Her whole flipping life, that's how long.

Would she trade this for something or somewhere more exciting? No, but it would be nice to have *someone* to share it with…besides the horses.

Footsteps on gravel snapped her attention away from the array of colors. "Patience?"

"Guess again," came Tanner's voice as he strode into view. He leaned against the barn door, hands in pockets, sunset at his back accenting his delectable profile. "Figured you'd be out here. Seems there're more horse farmers in the stable tonight than in houses. Except at Thistledown."

She stood. "There's a problem at Thistledown? Does Nathan need help?"

Tanner went inside and pulled up beside her. "My dear brother took a bubble bath."

"Oh my God, he's lost his mind. He's flipped. I knew it. The stress is too much for him."

"Not unless someone can get stressed out bathing." Tanner shrugged. "Though I doubt if much bathing actually took place."

She gave him a hard look, searching for signs of unbalance. "Have you been sipping moonshine again or is your brain still pickled from last night?"

"Nate and Savannah had the bubble bath. In Ravish-scented bubbles, no less. Now they're cuddling together in the barn to keep an eye on the horses."

Charity sat. Or did she fall? "Savannah's in a barn…with horses? She bought Ravish? Thought she settled on Bondage."

"Guess she was torn. If you think Savannah in a barn is a stretch, Nate in a bubble bath boggles the mind."

Charity grinned. "Guess I get to keep my pie."

Tanner took a seat beside her. The long shadows of early evening faded to soft gray and a breeze drifted inside, rippling in Tanner's chestnut hair.

"Yeah, Kentucky Girl, you get your pie." He massaged the back of his neck. "Bubble baths or not, I still don't think those two are suited for each other. This is just a novelty for Savannah."

"Trust me on this one, Tanner. Savannah in a barn is way beyond novelty. But—" she added quickly "—if you still think we should break up this engagement, I'm all for it."

He gave her a suspicious look. "You haven't done much to speed things along so far."

Oh, boy. She'd been afraid of this, that he wouldn't believe she was giving their partnership her best shot. "I'm thinking, I'm thinking."

His eyes turned to black satin. "We could think better with pie. I feel like I need some pie. Saw it in the middle of the kitchen table when I walked past the house. If we had pie and coffee, we could come up with some fine ways to break up Savannah and Nate. Besides, you don't want all that pie for yourself. Go straight to your hips and you have such…nice…"

The last word faded into the quiet as his gaze collided with hers, the two of them frozen in the moment. His breath felt warm as it fell across her cheeks. His lips parted…anticipating? She brushed a strand of hair from his forehead, her fingers trailing to his temple. In spite of all that kept them apart, he captivated her in every way. His handsome face, his strong build, his humor and leadership. Did she have any affect on him at all?

"I want you."

"What about the pie?" whispered Charity.

"To hell with pie."

Yeow, question answered. The warm spot deep inside her that had heated up the first time Tanner kissed her sparked to red-hot. "Thought we weren't the type for one-night stands."

His left brow arched and an easy grin tipped his lips. He slowly, deliberately, seductively stroked her arm, sending shock waves through her body. His voice was low and throaty as he said, "Charity, for once in our lives let's not try to control the situation."

Then he seized her lips with his—blistering, wild, demanding—and, suddenly, she didn't care if she ever controlled another thing in her whole life.

Heat emanated from him and flowed into her, making her warmer than she already was. His hand cupped her head in a possessive gesture, his fingers winding through her hair. His tongue connected with hers, stroking, encouraging, suggesting. Then he embraced her with his steely arm, brought her tight against his chest and gently rolled her back onto the bales.

She looked up at him. "How'd you do that?"

"Later."

Her heartbeat raced as she wrapped her arms around his neck, curling her fingers into his worn shirt to get closer still. His lips found the recesses of her throat and her head fell back, welcoming his advances.

He said, "You are incredible." He trailed a line of kisses to the back of her ear. She swooned, or whatever it was that women did when they felt weak.

"Where's your family." His left hand slid under her T-shirt, cupping her breast, making her head spin.

"What family?" The heat of his palm teased her nipple into a nub as a moan of pure delight wedged in her throat and her eyes wobbled in her head.

"Mama? Puck? Patience?" His tongue suckled her earlobe sending shivers down her spine.

"Sold them to the Gypsies."

"Good."

He slid her T-shirt up, along with her bra, and he sucked her breasts, first one then the other, making them swell with longing. She gasped and a surge of passion flooded through her, pooling between her legs.

She tugged his shirt from his jeans, needing to feel his skin. She ran her fingers up his firm sides and across the strong muscles of his back. She felt his fingers at the waistband of her jeans and he looked down at her, his gaze wild and hungry.

"You are an incredible woman. Beautiful, sexy, smart."

His words fell over her like a warm blanket, making her more desirous of him than before. Was that possible? No one had ever said these things to her before. "You should know I'm not exactly skilled at…this."

He grinned. "Double good. Makes it all the more fun."

Her fingers fought the buttons of his shirt, his the snap and zipper of his jeans. She pushed aside the denim and her hands wandered through the fine curls of hair that had driven her crazy the first time she'd seen him bare-chested. Then he stood and slowly slid her jeans and panties from her body.

TANNER'S HEART BEAT wildly; the passionate look in Charity's eyes mesmerizing him. She wanted him as much as he wanted her. He'd make this good for her. He slid down Charity's jeans, first revealing the smooth, silky-soft skin of her belly, the provocative indention of her navel, then the auburn curls between her legs. His erection strained against his own jeans and when he touched the soft, silky patch he could barely breathe. Urgency drove him on and he slid her jeans farther…until something stopped him. *Boots? Ah hell.* "Why couldn't you be barefoot?"

"Are you?"

She sat up and tugged them off, tossing one to the left and one to the right, then slid off her jeans and tossed them into the feed barrel. She looked up at him, grinning, her eyes full and round. She then undid his belt.

His heart raced as she unbuttoned and unzipped. Her fingers traced the length of his erection through his briefs. He fisted his hands as her strokes filled him with sweet agony. "Charity. I only have so much control. I've wanted this for…since I got here and—"

"You have?"

She glanced back to him as her hand cupped his hardness, the heat of her palm nearly sending him over the edge. He stepped back and yanked off his boots, almost losing his balance, then his jeans and briefs. He pulled her up and took her in his arms, kissing her lips, her eyes, her hair, and reveling in the feel of her skin against his—his erection cocooned in the softness of her abdomen, her breasts teasing his chest. "I want you so bad."

He laid her on the blanketed bails, then put himself on top of her. "Oh, damn, we can't do this."

"*What?*" Her eyes shot wide open. "You wait till *now* to figure out you don't want to—"

"Condom." He pushed himself from her, tripped on his own boots and fell. Kneeling, he rooted through his jeans' pockets, found his wallet and pulled out a crinkled blue package. He held it up like a trophy. "Old but not too old."

She sat up. "Need…help?"

He winked. "In a minute I will." He rolled on the protection, leaned her back on the blanket and bracing himself on his elbows, covered her body with his. "Now, where were we?" He kissed her. "Were we here?" He kissed her left nipple. "Or here?" He kissed the right. "Or here?"

A passionate gasp escaped her parted lips and he said, "I want to make this last, I really do, but—"

His words died as he felt her legs wrap around his back, bringing the heat of her desire to his. Pleasure roared through him like an out-of-control freight train. "Thought you weren't skilled."

Her eyes blazed, her breaths came faster. "I'm learning." She licked her lips, her legs tensed more. "Can we talk later? Hurry, okay?"

The pleasure building in him was unbearable as his hardness touched her softest place. He clenched his teeth till his jaw hurt, holding on to the last shreds of control, then slowly he eased himself into her. She was so tight, so hot, so wet, so incredibly perfect.

"Oh, Tanner." Her passionate cry echoed through the barn, driving his restraint over the edge. He filled her completely, then again and again, taking her and himself to an ecstasy he'd never experienced before.

CHARITY LAY perfectly still, her legs still molded around Tanner, his head nestled between her breasts.

She could feel his breathing slow as her fingers traced the muscles of his back. He was magnificent, in and out of bed, and she would remember him for-ever…even though he'd be many thousands of miles away. She shuddered at the thought of not having him near.

"Cold?"

"Just thinking."

"That never leads to anything good." He pushed himself up, gazing down at her. She ran her fingers over the cleft in his chin, her eyes not leaving his. Then she replaced her touch with a feather-light kiss, enjoying the roughness of his beard on her lips, then her tongue.

He kissed her, deeply, wetly, intimately, restoking the heat building again inside her.

He suddenly sat up, leaving her warmed body for the chill of evening. He raked his hair and shook his head. Was there a problem?

He grinned. "Well, damn, if that wasn't some great sex, Kentucky Girl."

"Huh?"

He disposed of the condom and grabbed his briefs.

Sex? "That's all this was to you was…*sex?*"

"Like you said, a fling's a bad idea, remember? Better get your clothes in case that family of yours escapes from the Gypsies."

She couldn't move if she had to. This was just a

romp in the hay? Actually, it was *on* the hay, but right now it didn't matter diddly. She sat up and glared at him as he pulled on one boot then the other.

He patted her on the head. *Patted her on the head?* How many women got their heads patted after lovemaking? None, that's how many.

"I better get going. Told some of the guys from high school I'd meet up with them for a beer or two." He glanced at his watch. "I'm late, but hey, it sure was fun."

He stood and dusted himself off. "Talk to you later. See if you can come up with any ways to break up Savannah and Nate, okay? You haven't been doing such a great job, you know." He turned and left.

Charity sat on the bails, nearly naked, watching Tanner's retreating figure till it faded into the darkness outside. She was going to kill him dead. Wring his neck with her jeans that had landed in the feed barrel, chop off his nether regions with a dull knife. The swine, jerk, butthead—

"Charity? You in there?" came Patience's voice from outside the barn.

Yikes. "I'm in here. I'll be out in a minute." She snatched her neck-wringing jeans and tugged them on. Grabbed her panties and shoved them into her right boot, then yanked down her bra and T-shirt as Patience strode in.

Patience flipped on the light and surveyed Charity's appearance. "What the heck happened to you?

Where're your boots? Didn't I just see Tanner leaving? He didn't look too happy."

He'd be a lot less *happy if I get a chance to take care of him like I want to.* Charity smoothed back her hair. "Tanner?" She wiggled her bare toes on the concrete. "Didn't see him. I...was...sleeping." She nodded to the bails. "There. Till you called. He must have seen me and left."

"You are so full of baloney." Patience's face split with a devilish wide grin and she chuckled. "I may be the youngest sister, but that doesn't make me a candidate for the stupid club, and though I have no idea how oats on your jeans play into all this, I'm sure there's one heck of a story connected to it."

She held up her hand as if warding off a stampede of horses and rushed on. "But, hey, if you don't want to tell me, that's fine. Kissing and telling is taboo." She looked around at the rumpled blanket and burst out laughing. "Taboo is an understatement and you don't have to say a word. I can pretty much connect the dots and—"

"Patience!" Charity pulled in a deep, steadying breath. "Why are you here, other than to harass the heck out of me?"

"Harassing you is my duty as a younger sister. Comes with the position." She waved a fistful of notepaper. "And the phone hasn't stopped ringing. Everybody wants Mama's yeast concoction. She made up some before she left, but not near enough."

"So?"

Patience spread her arms and rolled her eyes. "So we have to fill in. Make up some batches. No one reported any new sick horses today but…" She paused and looked out the open barn door. "I wonder if the rain yesterday had anything to do with that?"

"Why would rain keep horses from getting sick?"

Patience furrowed her brow. "I don't know, but as a scientist I can tell you there's no such thing as co-incidence in nature."

"You can give me a lecture on Biology 101 later. Right now we have a problem. We don't know how to make up Mama's concoction."

Patience stuck her nose in the air like some reining monarch. "Even some of the people who snubbed us when things weren't so good around here are calling. Can't wait to tell Mama that."

"By some miracle, did she give you the formula?"

"She just called with it because she got to thinking this might happen." Patience stroked her chin, a worry line creasing her forehead. "Puck was there."

"Well, of course he was. He drove, remember? A few hours ago we waved bye-bye?"

"They were having room service. I could hear the waiter in the background asking if he should pour the wine. Dinner, together in Mama's room. You don't think Mama and Puck are…*staying* in the same room, do you?"

''They're having dinner, they're hungry and thirsty. Now, where's this recipe?''

Patience handed it to her. She read over the ingredients and puffed out a breath of air. ''Well, we have enough yeast to make up one batch tonight, but tomorrow we'll have to get more supplies.''

''Mama says she gets the yeast from some supplier in Danville. How are we going get Mama's mixture to all these people—'' she waved the papers in the air ''—get to Danville for more yeast and make up more batches and distribute that before more horses get sick? Most of the farms are too busy with horses already sick to spend time coming here. And a lot of these places are hours away.''

Charity caught a glimpse of her white undies in the boot. She ground her teeth. She was never going to wear white undies again. Pat on the head? She'd give Tanner Davenport a pat on the head…with a two-by-four. ''I'll get our friendly neighborhood aviator and his magnificent flying machine to help us.''

''Did he say he would? How does he even know we need help?''

''Oh, he'll help, all right. All I need is some excuse—any old excuse will do—to drive a stake through his lily-livered heart.'' She kicked the boot— the one without the underwear—stubbing her toe but not really caring. ''Then again I couldn't drive a stake through that man's heart because that man doesn't have a heart.''

A wide-eyed Patience gaped at Charity. "*Whoa.*
Maybe what I think happened here between you and
Tanner didn't happen after all. I'll get together the
stuff that we need to make up Mama's concoction."

Charity nodded. "And tomorrow morning I'll get
Tanner's sorry hide out of bed at the crack of dawn
and get him to make himself useful for a change. He
may not like the Ridge, but since he's here, he's helping us whether he wants to or not."

TANNER KNEW HE WAS dreaming, but since that was
as close to Charity as he'd ever get again, he'd settle
for the dream. He held her close, his arms around her,
her red hair flying in the warm breeze, both of them
naked, riding Ranger and—

"Tanner Davenport, you no-good polecat, get up."
It was Charity, yelling. Why would she be yelling in
his dream? Especially about him being no good. Why
wasn't she telling him she wanted to make love with
him more than anything and—

"This isn't the Klondike, no hibernating."

She was banging on the door, or was that kicking
down the door? It was really loud. He squinted open
one eye as she bellowed, "There's work to be done."

He sat up and noticed the first glimpse of dawn
peeking over the hills outside the window. He tossed
off his covers and stood, rubbed the sleep from his
eyes, then opened them to see Charity standing in
front of him.

Holy hell. He was naked as the day he was born. He instinctively sat and grabbed the sheet to cover himself.

"Don't bother. I've seen it before and it ain't all that impressive." She threw his shirt and it landed on his head, sleeves flapping over his ears like giant muffs. "We need you and your aircraft to save the horses. And if you refuse, I intend to feed your bony carcass to the bears and—"

"Tell me what you want me to do. And, just for the record, there aren't any bears on the Ridge. And why are you so damn crabby this early in the morning?"

"Maybe because I've been up all night making Mama's yeast brew and I bet I could find a bear if I really tried. We need you to fly the preparation to the farms and to go to Danville to pick up new supplies. There isn't time to drive to all those places. So it's up to you."

He could see the fire in her eyes, but it didn't crowd out the fatigue or the hurt. He knew there'd be hurt when he'd given her that "damn great sex" line last night after they'd made love.

But what else could he do? Tell her how much he cared for her and one week later fly off into the sunset? "Damn great sex" seemed a much cleaner break. Fast, immediate, no complications. No need for a lot of explanations. When two people weren't meant to be together, there wasn't anything else to consider.

Then he took in her soft pink lips and wild hair and knew he lied. He folded his hands over the sheet to hide his immediate and soon-to-be obvious reaction to her. "I'll meet you at your place in an hour. I have to gas up the plane. Get what you need me to deliver to your south pasture, and I'll land there. Write out some directions with landmarks I can spot from the air. Tell me what you need at Danville. Better yet, call in the order and have it waiting at the airport. That'll save us time. I'll see if a few of Nate's hands can't come over to help you."

She peered down at him, hands on her hips. "Why are you so darn agreeable? Thought for sure I'd have to harangue you a lot more to get you to cooperate." She pulled a paper from her pocket and held it up. "I made a haranguing list. Why are you doing this of your own free will? You don't even like horses all that much, and people around here never meant that much to you. You said so yourself."

He thought, *Because I want to help make things easier for you. Just once take some of the worry and work off your shoulders.* But if he told her then she'd know he cared about her and that's the very thing he didn't want. What kind of caring person lasted a week, then left? Instead he said, "It'll give me something to do. A little action."

"Besides breaking up Savannah and Nathan?" She stood in front of him, not moving, looking more lovely than ever. "Didn't expect you to come around so easily.'' She raised her left brow. ''I was kind of looking forward to the bear thing.''

''I could tell.''

As much as he wanted to, they *couldn't* make love again. If they did he'd never get her out of his mind and the cold nights in Alaska would be longer, lonelier than ever.

Chapter Eight

Tanner flew the Cessna over the mountains as he thought about those damn long Alaskan nights waiting for him. Maybe that's why he couldn't keep his mind off Charity, all warm and soft and giving under him the previous night, making love to him. He thought of her dreams and the dog-with-a-bone perseverance she used to achieve them. He'd miss her back in Alaska. Miss her like hell…and not just between his sheets.

But she sure wasn't coming with him to the land of ice and snow—what would she do, raise polar bears? And he sure wasn't staying. What would he do, knit horse blankets?

He banked away from the afternoon sun hovering at the crest of the hills and headed for MacKay Farms for the third time that day. He'd delivered the yeast from Danville and come back two more times to pick up more orders for Mama's mixture, then delivered those. Charity and Patience and Savannah had worked flat-out to get the deliveries ready. Savannah up to her elbows in grain and yeast? Now there was a surprising picture.

Sunlight hit the hillside perfectly, accenting the fresh green foliage and the spots of silver sprinkled through the trees. One of the joys of flying, it showed the whole picture.

He yawned and adjusted the flaps, then brought the Cessna down with a gentle bounce, landing in the south pasture. He taxied the plane to the side, got out and headed for the house. Coffee, he needed some of the high-octane stuff before he made another run.

He spied Charity as he passed the second barn. She sat on the bales of hay they'd made love on yesterday, staring into a mug of something steamy. He thought of the steam they had created there, which was a lot more potent than the single curl of vapor rising from the mug now. But there'd be no more steam, not even a little simmer. It was finished. Better that than getting them both into something that had *impossible* written all over it.

He started for the main house until she stopped him with, "You made that last run fast enough. Aren't you worried about the skyway patrol giving you a ticket?"

Her hair was pulled back into a sagging ponytail; she was slack-shouldered, dog-tired. He sat beside her, took the mug from her fingers, lingering just a second to enjoy the warmth of her touch. Then he drank long and deep, keeping his mind on the brew instead of Charity. He wiped the back of his hand across his mouth. "Dang. That's got to be the worst coffee I ever had."

"It's tea. Savannah made it. She signed up for cooking lessons at the adult ed center yesterday. Our prayers have been answered. I hope."

He leaned against the side of the barn, the coolness of the wood pressing into his shoulders. It relieved the strain from hours in the cockpit and the heat that started to build inside him whenever he was around Charity.

Escaped tendrils of hair kissed the back of her neck and he'd give anything to do the same. "What do you want me to deliver next?"

"How about some good news. Seems like it's been a long time since I heard any. More horses getting sick and no one knowing why."

She nodded toward the back of the barn. "Black Button didn't eat much today. His eyes aren't as bright as usual. And one more of Nathan's is sick."

"That's pretty much the story wherever I went." He wanted to feel her in his arms, offer some support, be there when she needed someone. But then what? *Whoops, sorry, baby, I'm heading home to Alaska.*

She looked at him. "I have your money."

"For…?"

"The yeast. When I called Danville to get the bill, they said you took care of it."

He waved his hand in the air. "Forget it." He stared at the mug, trying to ignore his desire for her. Maybe if he thought about something else. "This sure tastes like coffee. Maybe Savannah's on to something. She could call it tea-offie."

"I think that's toffee. The name's already taken, and you're a little loopy." She stood and looked down at him. "Go home and get some sleep, and I'm not forgetting about the money. I'll write you a check."

"I'll tear it up." He lay down on the bails, balancing the mug on his chest, studying the ceiling in the fading light. "You have a bird nest in the rafters. Wren, I think. I'm going to rest here for a little while. Wake me in time for Christmas dinner, okay? Any time before that is way too soon."

He closed his eyes, feeling his fatigue drain away. He wanted to be here, on the hay where they'd made love this time last night. He could almost feel her body next to his, her legs around him, him buried inside her. "Can I have these bales? A souvenir of…Kentucky…to take back to Alaska. I can load them into the Cessna and—"

"Go to sleep, Tanner."

He felt her lift the mug from his chest and drop a blanket over him, the same one they'd made love on. He could smell Charity's freshness trapped in the folds, and he wanted to make love to her all over again. "Can I have the blanket, too?"

She stroked his cheek, he'd recognize her touch anywhere. Her voice was soft and low as she said, "I get the blanket."

All the tea or coffee in the world, no matter how rotten it tasted, wouldn't make him forget Charity and how much he wanted her and couldn't have her. He'd think about something else, dream about something else. Flying. He could always dream of flying. And he had to do that or he'd wake up more frustrated than a frog in a dry pond.

CHARITY WATCHED the steady rise and fall of Tanner's chest slow into the deep rhythm of sleep. He'd worked so hard, dropping off supplies, delivering the mixture to the horse farmers. And it cost him, not just for the supplies he'd picked up, but for the gas. A plane didn't just flap its wings and take off. He stirred under the blanket and she thought of last night. Great sex? To her it had been much more.

He was loyal, dependable, hardworking. A little lacking in the sincerity department, but he'd taken on responsibilities that day with no hesitation and it probably didn't have much to do with her threat of feeding him to the bears. Maybe it was best he thought of their lovemaking as just sex, because if it meant something more to him—as much as it meant to her—then his leaving would be beyond awful.

She headed for the house as dusk settled in, the kitchen lights beckoning. "What's cooking?" she asked Savannah as she pulled up next to the counter-top. She held her breath and prayed for peanut butter and jelly. Even Savannah couldn't botch that.

Savannah's apron was neat, her blond hair and makeup perfect. The twenty-first century June Cleaver, except for the cooking part. "Smells… different." So much for P.B. and J.

Savannah beamed. "Lasagna. Pork chop lasagna. We didn't have any ground beef or cheese, but we did have those wide noodle things and tomato soup. So I substituted. Where's Tanner? Thought I heard his plane land."

"Sleeping out in the barn. I think he's comatose."

Savannah nodded. "Well, it's no wonder, since he made all those deliveries and brought that little foal into the vet in Louisville. Oh, and he got Mrs. Chandler the diabetes medicine her son forgot to pick up because he's got all those sick horses and—"

"When did all this happen and how'd *you* know about it?"

Savannah broke lettuce into a colander. "Patience told me before she went into town to do some research at the library on gymnosperms?"

She narrowed her eyes and put down the lettuce. "Sounds kind of…sexy. Think it has anything to do with athletic sperm? Guess it's too much to hope Patience is studying something besides roots and leaves and—"

"I think it has something to do with trees. Now what about Tanner?"

Savannah picked up the lettuce and sighed. "That's what I was afraid of. You'd think as a biology major she'd have a little more interest in *human* biology, especially the man part. And—"

"What about Tanner?"

"Well, you know Patience manned the phones all day and talked to everyone. So she got the scoop on what's going on."

Savannah grinned at Charity. "Tanner was a hero around here today. Talk of the town. Isn't he wonderful."

Charity sat on the nearest bar stool and stared at Savannah. Yeah, Tanner was a hero and Savannah appreciated him, admired him, and was so very much like him—except she had a much better wardrobe. She loved adventure, would go anywhere—*could* go anywhere. She wasn't afraid to tackle anything. Pork chop lasagna proved that much. And she was beautiful and witty. "What do you think of Alaska?"

She laughed and hugged her hands to her chest. "Wouldn't you just love to see it? All the bears, glaciers, eagles and—"

"You should marry Tanner."

Savannah dropped the whole head of lettuce into the colander. Bug-eyed, she sat on the stool beside Charity. Her mouth opened and shut, then opened again, but nothing came out. Her lipstick smudged.

Nothing on Savannah ever smudged. Wouldn't dare. Finally she said, "What did you say?"

Charity pulled in a deep breath. "I've got to tell you something, something important. I've been a terrible sister. Horrible, actually. If you want to yell and scream at me, I understand, and I can even suggest some appropriate adjectives. You can start with conniving and sneaky and—"

"Charity, you are the best sister anyone could ever have."

Charity rolled her eyes. "I'm trying to confess here, Savannah. Enjoy the moment. You'll have something to lord over me for the rest of our lives. Think of the advantages. Forever you'll be able to say, 'Remember that time you—'"

"What in the world are you talking about? You're not making any sense."

"Yeah, well it's going to make sense, and it ain't going to be pretty." She took Savannah's hand. "I've been keeping you and Tanner apart because I was afraid he'd be a temptation to you with his Tales of the Last Frontier and you'd get all excited and instead of marrying Nathan you'd go off on some adventure of your own somewhere."

"You thought I'd go off with Tanner?" Her brows arched to her hairline.

"When he first got here, I didn't think so. I just thought you'd go off. You know, like you did to L.A. and New York. But now..." She stood and paced.

She studied the cracks in the linoleum and continued. "Now that I think about it, you're perfect for Tanner. And he's perfect for you. He's wonderful, he really is. He'll take care of you. You'll have fun and life will never be boring and you'll laugh and he'll tell you things you never knew about. You'll have kids and dogs that pull sleds and you'll love it and…"

She looked back at Savannah. She grinned like a cat dropped in a pitcher of cream. "You're in love with Tanner Davenport."

This time Charity's brows shot up to *her* hairline. "No, no, no. That's not what I said at all. It's you and Tanner who belong together. Nathan will get over it in time. He'll understand it's for the best. This has absolutely nothing to do with me. Can you think of two more opposite people than me and Tanner Davenport?"

Savannah laughed as she bobbed her head. "Of course, I can. Me and Nathan. And I love Nathan with all my heart and soul, and he would never, ever, understand me running off with his brother because Nathan and I are head over heels in love with each other, and we both know it."

Charity heaved a sigh and reclaimed the stool next to Savannah. "Guess this means you and Tanner aren't getting hitched anytime soon, huh?"

Savannah grinned. "I already have my man." She held up her hand, the diamond sparkling in the overhead light. "Now it's your turn. You're beautiful and desirable and you need to start feeling that way."

"Me?"

"Of course, you. If you could see the way Tanner looks at you when you're not looking at him you'd realize just how much he wants you."

"Thought I had this all figured out. You and Tanner, I mean."

"For once, dear sister, you don't. You missed by a mile."

Charity propped her elbow on the counter and rested her head in her palm. "Well, nothing's going on between me and Tanner. I'm sure of that. The Ridge is his least favorite place on earth and he doesn't care for me at all—not the way two people care about each other if something's ever going to happen between them." She wrinkled her nose. "That much I got straight from the horse's mouth."

"Sometimes the horse doesn't know what he wants. Don't throw this away, Charity. You deserve happiness. We all do. Being married to that creep Billy Ray made me realize that and appreciate Nathan even more. Tanner can make you happy just as Nathan makes me deliriously happy. Tanner cares for you, I can tell. I know these Davenport men. They're a breed all their own. Tough, hardheaded, single-minded and honorable. Always honorable."

Savannah smiled. "There's room for a double wedding. Two sisters, two brothers. Could be fun. You should think about it.''

This was how the MacKay women had gotten through some pretty tough times over the years. They loved each other and gave selflessly. Charity kissed her sister on the cheek. ''One week from today is your wedding day and for you to even offer to share it is the most wonderful gift you could give me.''

''I wish I could give you a barn full of healthy horses.''

Charity pulled in a deep breath. ''Me, too. And that you could do the same for Nathan and the rest of the farms on the Ridge. Of all the horse towns in Kentucky, the Ridge seems to be the hardest hit. Think because we're up here problems would circle around us and let us alone. It's only a matter of time before we start losing horses. The yeast mixture is just buying us time. It works for a short while, then the horses stop eating altogether. I don't know what we're going to do, Savannah. I really don't.''

Savannah wiped away a tear from Charity's face. She hadn't realized she'd been crying. Savannah took her hand, tears welling in her own eyes.

Charity said, ''This is not the way I wanted your pre-wedding week to go. I'm so sorry.''

''Nathan and I will get married. All we need is five minutes in front of the preacher. I wouldn't dream of making Nathan take part in a big extravagant wedding with everything he has on his mind now. All I want is Nathan in my life.''

Another tear slid down Charity's face; this one she felt and couldn't have stopped it if she'd wanted to. ''You're a good girl, Savannah MacKay.''

Savannah grinned, showing her perfect white teeth. ''I know.''

The back screen door slammed and the sound of boots tramping through the screened-in-porch and across hardwood came their way. Tanner stood in the doorway between the hall and kitchen, bleary-eyed, hair like a Chia Pet, shirttail half in and half out, handsome as all get-out. Charity's heart went to two hundred beats per minute just looking at him. Darn.

''Got a flashlight?'' he asked.

Charity pointed to the overhead fixture. ''Electricity. Even got it in the barn. Just flip the switch and you're in business.''

He shook his head as if waking up. ''I need to take a ride into the pasture with a flashlight.''

Charity quickly wiped her cheeks in case any tears remained.

''Are…are you crying?'' Tanner's eyes widened, nearly covering his face.

''Of course not. I don't cry. Doesn't solve a thing.'' She went to Tanner and took his strong hand in hers and tugged him into the kitchen. She nudged him onto a stool, not wanting to let go of him but knowing it was for the best. ''You need to go home, to the cottage, get some real sleep in a real bed. You're losing it, flyboy.''

He raked his hair. ''When I'm flying in the afternoon, I see silvery patches in the trees. I don't remember seeing them years ago when I flew the biplane. Or if I did see, they didn't make an impression.''

She quirked her brow. ''Tomorrow everything will be clearer. There's electricity in the cabin. Need some aspirin? Maybe you should consider glasses.''

''It's something in nature, bird nests maybe… It's hard to tell. I remember a lot of things about the Ridge, especially from the sky. Heck, I've made two perfect emergency landings and a boatload of deliveries and not gotten lost once. I remember this place better than I thought I did.''

She held up three fingers in front of his eyes. ''How many?''

''My vision's fine.''

''Tanner, I ride the pastures every day, every season. There's nothing out there but fence and grass like every other year. Lots of both. And the horses. Maybe a buzzard flies by occasionally because we're on the hilltop, but that's it.''

He shook his head. ''You can't see the differences from the ground. You have to be up high where you can see more at one time.'' He looked around the kitchen. ''Where's a flashlight?''

''You just figured this out?''

He shrugged. "I kind of dreamed about it."

"And I thought I needed a life," she said more to herself than him. No need to worry about *her* haunting *his* dreams as he haunted hers. He dreamed of…trees? She was now, officially, behind trees in Tanner's dreams. Bet Britney Spears was never behind trees in a man's dreams.

She continued, "What makes you think this silvery stuff has anything to do with the horses getting sick if it's in the trees? Last time I checked, horses didn't climb worth diddly. They jump pretty good, but they really suck at climbing. Besides, the horses could be getting sick from a lot of things. The water, the air."

"I won't sleep till I check this out. It'll only take a few hours, and if I find something I can get it to Mama Kay in the morning. You don't have to come along. I know the way to the pasture, been there enough. If I don't find what I'm looking for, I'll head on over to Thistledown and snoop around there. It's positioned a little higher on the Ridge, gets a little more sunlight. Maybe that is why Nate's horses are more affected than yours."

Charity said, "It's dark out now. You won't see much. A flashlight is useless."

"I'll take Patience along. Maybe she knows what this is. It's right up her alley."

"Plant Woman is in town at the library and you don't want her taking you anywhere. You'll never find your way back. When God was handing out senses of direction, Patience was last in line.''

Savannah pulled her pork chop lasagna from the oven and said, ''Charity should go with you. You don't know where the trees are. It's not like they line the whole fence. Besides, who would be around to harass you if you find nothing but grass and crickets?''

Savannah whipped off her apron with a flourish and draped it over the counter. She put a lid on the casserole. ''I'm going to Thistledown. Told Nathan I'd cook dinner. He loves my cooking.''

Tanner slid Charity a quick look that suggested Nathan didn't realize what he was in for this time.

Savannah winked at Charity. ''Don't get lost out there.''

''I didn't say I was going.'' And she hoped love was not only blind but didn't have taste buds.

Savannah's smile turned up a notch as she said to Charity, ''You'll go, it's your farm.'' She grinned at Tanner. ''Good luck, and I mean that on many levels.''

STARS DOTTED THE HEAVENS and a three-quarter moon lit the way as Tanner opened the gate into the pasture then slid home the latch after he and Charity had entered. Why in the world had he let her come? He must have been nuts to agree. Having her right beside him without touching her was torture. This was not the way to keep her out of his life and out of his mind.

"Beautiful night," she said.

And it was, but Charity was more beautiful. She seemed so much a part of this place he couldn't imagine her anywhere else.

"I see your leather jacket survived our trek in the rain."

"Been through worse than rain." He pulled a KitKat from his pocket so he would have something else to do besides think of Charity. "Want some?"

She pulled a disk of peppermint from her own pocket. "I'll stick with these."

"Stomach problems?"

"With so much at stake, every horse farmer on the ridge is popping mints."

And there was a lot on the line, especially for Charity. Her whole life she'd worked for this season, and now sickness threatened to blow it all to hell and back.

He slid the chocolate from the wrapper as she asked, "Dinner?"

"Better than what Nate's getting. Savannah's no Martha Stewart. Maybe the cooking lessons will help. This time we didn't have to come up with some way of breaking up the wedding. Savannah's pork chop lasagna might do the trick all by itself."

"Nathan's not looking for a Martha Stewart."

He considered that as he took another bite. "I wonder what he *is* looking for?"

He glanced at her and noticed a smile slowly trip across her lips. "Love. Complete and eternal. Isn't that what everyone wants?"

Was it? Maybe. Probably. But was it enough? Probably not. There had to be something else to build on, like a little something in common.

The soft plodding of the horses' hooves on the damp grass mixed with creaks of leather and animals scurrying in the bush hoping for a late-night snack. "Does this mean you think the wedding should happen and our partnership is dissolved?" Tanner asked.

She faced him. "Nope, it's a good partnership. Works like a charm." She waved her hand over the pasture. "And now that we're out here instead of sleeping, where do you want to go? Where did you see this…silvery stuff? You been reading a lot of Stephen King lately?"

"I've seen the patches from the sky, kind of hidden in with the new leaves, so I don't know where it is from down here. It's not under all the trees, just some."

"Some? Like which ones?"

"Like it's hard to tell a couple hundred feet above ground. Let's try by the fences, the trees hanging into the pasture. The horses are grazing in the pastures, so if it is something tree-related that's getting them sick it has to be trees in the pasture."

''Whatever you say. This is your party. There's a clump of hickories up ahead.''

Tanner nudged his horse into a trot, following Ranger across the pasture. Charity was one with that horse, moving as she moved in perfect harmony. Then Tanner remembered how Charity had moved with him, when they'd made love, the two of them together in complete unison.

Every muscle in his body hardened at the memory, even his blood felt hot, and he was thankful for the cover of night to conceal his painful state. They pulled up to the fence and he dismounted, hoping he wouldn't fall. Not only would it hurt like hell, he'd have to explain why.

''You're looking kind of clumsy there. Are you okay? You should have eaten some dinner.''

No, he wasn't okay and his condition wouldn't improve no matter how much dinner he ate. Charity in moonlight looked incredible. ''Maybe you should ride on back. You've got to be tired. I could be out here for hours.''

He held his breath, wishing she'd agree and knowing she wouldn't. Turning back was not something Charity MacKay did.

''I'm here now. Besides, you've got me curious.''

He took the flashlight from his jacket pocket and cast into the trees. ''I'm hoping if I shine the light on this nest thing, it will show up.''

''Nothing but branches.''

He picked at the bark. "Brown." He shook his head. "Let's try some other trees."

"If something was going on, wouldn't Patience or Mama have noticed it?"

"They weren't looking for a problem. It's spring in Kentucky, like it is every other year. The thing is, I haven't seen it for a while. I sort of have a fresh eye."

She remounted. "Come on, there's an old oak in the middle of the pasture. If that's affected, all my horses are doomed because they love to graze under it."

Tanner followed her to the oak and dismounted, more aware of his horny condition than ever. He looked at the moon through the spidery still-bare limbs. It was different from the tranquility of Alaska. The hills of Kentucky were not the untouched rawness of the Yukon but more a promise of man to nature, to protect and cherish a wonderful gift. "Bet this tree's been here since before you were born."

"Great-granddaddy MacKay planted it when he came here from Scotland. Nobody knew horses like he did. They say he could tell a champion foal at birth. Feel it in his bones. Sure could use his input these days."

She gazed back at the tree. "It looks just the same this year as it has every other year, dark bark, no silver in sight."

They walked back across the pasture to the fence

line leading their horses. The moon dipped behind puffs of clouds, the earth smelled warm and rich now that the cold months of winter had ended. Silence settled around them as if they were the only people on earth. Having Charity at his side felt perfect to Tanner. Her arm brushed his, then his brushed hers, and he knew if he didn't kiss her he'd die. He stopped by a clump of smaller trees at the fence.

"See something here?" she asked.

Yeah, he saw her, and what she did to him was damn sinful. Desire kicked common sense to the curb. Kissing her was a really bad idea and he should start walking away, look for whatever was in the trees and not touch Charity. Because one touch and he'd be a goner.

Hell, who was he kidding? He already was a goner.

He backed her against the brown slats of the fence, a shallow canopy of tiny new leaves cascading around her like a trickling waterfall. He touched her silky hair, reveling in the texture before he tucked it behind her ear; he gently tipped her chin, bringing her face to his.

Her skin had the gentle radiance of alabaster, her eyes brilliant, unfathomable, compelling. Her mouth parted a fraction, his insides ignited and he brushed her soft, sweet lips with his own, exhilarated by the feel of her hot breath mixing with his.

He kissed her softly, giving her a chance to back away. When she didn't, he swooped her into his embrace, bringing her body to his, and he kissed her hard and long, wanting it to never end. Her breasts swelled against his chest and his throbbing desire for her pressed hard against her.

She tasted wonderful, delicious, as mint united with chocolate. Her tongue mated with his, implying the very thing he wanted. He twisted his fingers into her amazing hair and trailed kisses from her lips to the nape of her neck.

"We can't do this." Her voice was ragged, throaty, strained.

"I know." He planted kisses behind her left ear.

She pulled her head back and stared up at him, dreamy-eyed, her breathing fast and shallow. "To you this is just fun and games, but to me it's something more. I can't get involved with you, Tanner, because…" Her eyes cleared, then narrowed. "Because there's something in my hair."

She touched her head. "And it's furry and it's moving. *What is it! What is it!*"

She shoved him away, bent her head, shook it like a rag doll, and ran her hands through her hair as she jumped around in circles.

"Hold still."

"Do something!"

He snagged her around the waist and held her tight. Her shaking head whacked his jaw, making him see stars for a second. Her elbow caught him right in the ribs.

Trying to hold her with one arm, he flipped on the flashlight and studied the top of her head, following its erratic movements. Her red hair was dotted with silver, and he plucked out something…fuzzy?

"Look," he said, holding it in front of her so she could see.

She stilled. "It's a caterpillar."

"Cute little guy. Black head, brown stripe. That's what's in your hair."

She screamed and shook her head more.

"Since when are you afraid of caterpillars?"

"Since they're in my hair!"

Guess he shouldn't have pointed out the black head and brown stripe.

"If you hold still for a second, I'll get them out."

"Them?" She screeched.

"Guess the gooey stuff must be part of their co-coon."

Charity shook her head and pulled at her hair. At this rate she'd go bald.

Her head jabbed his right eye. Dang. He'd been in bar fights that weren't this rough. Never in all his days did he think he'd get beat up at the MacKay Farms, owned and operated by four beautiful Southern women, who were completely peaceful…well, most of the time they were peaceful.

Chapter Nine

Tanner watched Charity in the moonlight, head wagging, hands flailing, legs kicking. Maybe he shouldn't have told her about the cocoon, either. "Don't panic. It's just some webby stuff and it will wash out of your hair."

"What about now? And the caterpillars are on my jacket. Lots of them." She wiped at her front, knocking them to the ground. "Check my back." She turned around, the canopy of leaves brushing against her. "Are they there?"

Oh, boy. A furry line stretched and bent its way across her shoulders. He brushed them off as another one dropped into her hair, then on to his sleeve.

He didn't say one word—*lesson learned*—pulled her from under the low tree and plucked the caterpillars from her hair.

"Did you get them all?"

"Absolutely." He hoped. He scanned her with the flashlight. "I pronounce you caterpillar free."

She flicked one from the collar of his jacket. "Why didn't they get in *your* hair?"

"They're looking for victims with the loudest screams." He smiled easily. "They succeeded."

She studied the tree. "I was the one under the limbs, you weren't. The little darlings are in there." She pointed a stiff, accusing finger.

She pulled off a young leaf. "It's a cherry tree. Black cherry. Patience just planted some by the house."

"Perhaps you should reconsider." Tanner glanced over her shoulder as she turned the leaf from front to back. "Caterpillars aren't unusual. They're always out. Nate and I used to have races with them."

He directed the flashlight into the tree sparsely covered with new growth. "The bark seems to be... moving?"

"Whoa, there must be a zillion caterpillars on that tree."

"And cocoons. That's what I saw from the plane. When the afternoon sun hits them, they turn silver."

Charity wiped her hand over her face. "This is all very interesting and a little itchy and darn inconvenient, but does this have anything to do with the horses getting sick? It's caterpillars like every other year."

Tanner shrugged. "Maybe nothing. Maybe everything. But I'm willing to bet there's a heck of a lot more of them this year than other years or I wouldn't have noticed their cocoons. We need to get some of these fuzzy guys to Patience to see what she thinks. Then we should call Mama Kay.''

Well, hell, it was back to business. Horse business. He pulled his army knife from the pocket of his bomber jacket and cut a branch from the cherry tree. He wrapped the branch along with some grass inside the jacket and tied the arms together.

Charity held up the package. ''Waterproof, one size fits all, contains stuff for every occasion and you don't leave home without it. It's a purse that you wear.''

Her hair had that stuck-my-finger-in-an-outlet look, but he realized he'd find her attractive no matter what she did to her hair. Was that anything like Nathan not caring how Savannah cooked? Hmm.

He carefully tucked the coat under his arm. ''You'd actually put caterpillars in your purse?''

''*Ugh.* You got me on that one.''

''Let's get these critters home before they develop a taste for leather instead of cherry.''

A HALF HOUR LATER Charity stood in the middle of the kitchen. She put her hands to her hips and frowned. ''We have caterpillars running around our floor. Mama would have a canary.''

Patience sat cross-legged on the linoleum and scooped up one light-haired furry caterpillar, then another. ''They're on a cookie sheet and not exactly running. They're really cute, maybe I should change my major.''

Tanner sat on a bar stool, munching on a fried chicken leg, and said to Patience, ''So what do you think about these little critters?''

She sat back and watched the furries slink around. ''*Malacosoma Americanum* is—''

''Translation please,'' Charity interrupted.

''The Eastern Tent Caterpillar, also referred to as E.T.C., is the larva stage of certain moths who lay their eggs in fruit trees. In the spring the eggs hatch and develop into the pupa stage, or caterpillar, and eventually form silky cocoons and—''

''Okay, okay.'' Charity held up her hands in surrender. ''This is great information and all, but what in the name of Zeus's armpit does this have to do with sick horses? *That's* what we want to know.''

Patience stuck her tongue out at Charity. ''I'm getting to that, if you would just give me a minute. Tanner has seen a lot of the cocoons from the air, and the weather is dry, giving the caterpillars a good chance to survive. And we have a lot of sick horses. Since there are no coincidences in science, there's a connection between these three things somewhere.'' She shot Charity a twisted smile. ''So, I suggest we do what all great scientists do when they need help.''

''Do tests?''

''Call their mother.''

Charity kept watch on the herd roaming the cookie

sheet as Patience called Mama on the phone in the den. Charity held a furry in her hand and said to Tanner, "They're not so bad when they're not crawling around in your hair and down your back."

"Heard Alvena had another horse come down with whatever this is."

Every muscle in Charity's body ached. Maybe from fatigue, probably from the sense of helplessness that ate at her insides like a sickness. She put the furry back on the sheet. "Every phone call brings more bad news, horses going from bad to worse. I don't know where this is all going to end. No one does." She looked at Tanner. "I'm glad you're here."

He stopped chewing. "Why? What I know about horses you can put on the back of a postage stamp."

"You flew all over the Ridge today, paid for the yeast with your own money, and I heard what you did for the foal and Mrs. Chandler's medication. You didn't have to do any of those things."

"Ha, you were just aching for an excuse to feed me to those bears."

This brought a smile. She needed a smile right now. "You still sit a horse like you were born on one. Raising horses may not be what you want to do with you life, but it suits you."

She sat on the stool next to Tanner's and put her hand on his leg, wanting to feel him and to add sincerity to what she said. "You could have taken over one of the best horse farms in the state, but you had to do what you had to do. I respect that, even though I don't understand it.''

''Sure you do.''

She arched her brow in question.

''Hell, Charity, you follow your dreams every bit as much as I do. When things were tough, you could have sold MacKay Farms and bailed out. Bet Billy Ray would have snapped it up in a heartbeat. Probably one of the reasons he married Savannah was to get his clutches into the place. Bet he was the one who suggested the fifty acres to divorce Savannah. You could have moved the family to town, got a regular job, lived a comfortable life.''

''And then I'd be horseless. I was horseless once, Tanner, for five long years, and it sucked rotten eggs.''

He took her hand in his and studied it. ''Guess that's like me being without a plane. I can't imagine not having a plane or two and taking off whenever I wanted to.''

Patience came back into the kitchen, a frown on her face. She didn't say anything but just stood there like a mannequin.

''Well?'' Charity asked, letting go of Tanner and missing the physical connection to him more than she thought possible. ''What did Mama say? Are the caterpillars off the hook? Not guilty? Give.''

''Puck was with her.''

''We've been through this. They're together in

Lexington. He drove. More than likely Mama read aloud the latest issue of *Thoroughbred Monthly;* they probably ate at Bob Evans off the senior citizens menu. What did she say about the blasted caterpillars? In case you didn't notice, we need some answers here.''

"They had a picnic in an orchard, under flowering apple blossoms. She said they noticed the tent caterpillars there, too.'' Patience cut her eyes to Charity. "They had wine and cheese and watched the sun set.''

Charity summoned all her self-control to keep from thumping Patience on her scientific back and yelling, *Caterpillars, think caterpillars. "Just spit out what Mama said!''*

Patience rolled her eyes. "All right, all right. She said we should bring what we have to her ASAP. The vets are working twenty-four/seven, so the sooner we get to her the better. She'll take them to the labs for tests.''

Charity nodded at Patience. "You should go.''

"Me? I'm a lowly biology student. What the heck do I know about anything?''

"You have some pretty neat Latin names for caterpillars and cherry trees and you're a lot more qualified than the rest of us. You and Tanner can tell the vets what they need to know about things around here. He's the one who got us on to this.''

Tanner stood and draped his arm around Patience.

"Guess this means me and my copilot here are flying to Lexington tonight. He looked down at her. "You know, you'd love Alaska. Lots of trees, big weeds. Insects the size of small dogs. No sisters telling you what to do. Dandelions grow two feet high in Juneau, and there are ten men for every woman." He rumpled her hair. "Not that you'd care about that."

A devilish grin played at the corners of Patience's lips. And a twinkle in her eyes? No grins and twinkles, Charity pleaded to any powers that be who were listening at the moment. At this rate she'd get Savannah married off, then have to start worrying about Patience.

Patience said, "Of course I don't care. All I want is to get my Ph.D."

Well, thank heavens for that. Charity didn't need any more men problems in the MacKay family. Nathan and Savannah. She and Tanner.

She and Tanner? She looked at him and her heart did a little flip. More like a big double somersault right off a high diving board. Not that it counted for much because there was no *she and Tanner,* except for that great sex part.

THE NEXT AFTERNOON midday sun poured into the entrance of the MacKay's foaling barn as Tanner strolled through the wide-open arched double doors. He yawned, thankful for the few hours of sleep he'd grabbed in Lexington before he and Patience returned.

Off-key humming came from the back stalls. Charity. He knew so much about her, the little things. He knew that she hummed and talked to the horses, that she liked tea instead of coffee, the way her hand fit in his, the feel of her fingers on his skin. And he knew the second she came into any room where he was, and the way she looked at him with hunger in her eyes when she thought he wasn't paying attention. He'd miss those little things. Hell, he'd miss the big thing, too—making love to her.

He found her in Misty Kay's stall, pitchfork in hand, tossing fresh hay from a pile as Mama Misty, full and round, waited patiently. He said, "Glad to see someone's holding down the fort while Patience and I were off lollygagging in the big city."

"Tanner?" Her head snapped around and she faced him. Damn he'd missed her. He'd been gone for a whopping sixteen hours and he'd missed her more than he thought possible.

"Why are you here? Why aren't you in Lexington? I didn't expect you back so soon." She came out of the foaling stall.

"Just landed at Thistledown and drove Patience home." He leaned against an upright beam and stuffed his hands into his pockets, enjoying having her so near. He watched her scoop a mound of hay as she'd probably done a million times before…then she dumped it on his head.

She hadn't done *that* a million times before. He

righted and wiped hay from his face. "What the hell was that for?"

Shafts fluttered down around him, sticking in his hair, eyebrows, ears and lips, slithering into his shirt, itching like mad.

"For not calling me, you big oaf. Blast your Alaskan hide. You stand here all calm and complacent as if you just came back from the Bahamas. You could have phoned. There are phones in Lexington. You know I'm worried into a stupor. It was *my* hair the caterpillars dropped into. That gives me certain rights and—"

"I did call and I got the answering machine. You need to get a phone out here. Besides, all you had to do was turn on the TV."

She wiped the hay from his shoulders and off his shirt. It was worth getting dumped on just to have her touch him. She continued, "Guess Savannah turned on the machine before she went to see Nate. And what's TV got to do with this?"

"Mama Kay and the scientist issued a tentative statement. Preliminary tests point to the caterpillars being guilty by quantity."

She stopped brushing. "That doesn't make one bit of sense."

"If you look at the whole picture, it does. There are a ton more of the furry guys this spring because of the lack of rain and abundance of cherry trees. They eat the leaves, releasing the cyanide and—"

"Cyanide?" She dropped the pitchfork to the concrete floor where it landed with a resounding clank.

"There's cyanide in cherry leaves—guess that's why there's no such thing as cherry leaf salad. Anyway, the poison gets into their systems and their droppings, which fall into the grass and get eaten by the horses. They can ward off some of the poison as they have in other years but not such large quantities."

"And nobody paid much attention because they're used to seeing them around in the spring."

"Bingo. And the ridge is high and dry. Now we have to cut down the cherry trees around the pastures and limit grazing till the caterpillars turn into moths and we get some good rains to wash away the droppings. Your mother and Puck should be home tomorrow. She's a media star, the darling of Kentucky. Has the reporters wrapped around her little finger. They'll probably make her a Kentucky Colonel."

"Do they have women Kentucky Colonels?"

"If they don't, they will now."

Tears pooled in Charity's eyes and his heart squeezed into a tight knot. He touched her cheek. The horses, this farm, her family were her life.

"It's over, Charity. At least, the worst part of it. Everything's going to be okay because now we know what we're dealing with and can fix it."

Her face lit up brighter than fireworks on the Fourth of July. She jumped into his arms, surprising the hell out of him, the action thumping the back of his head on the beam he'd been leaning against. She rained kisses on his cheeks, forehead, nose and chin. Then she kissed him full on the lips, making his blood flow hot with wanting her.

Okay, he could handle this. She was happy, a little exuberant. He could *want* her, he just couldn't *have* her, *again,* and kissing wasn't *having her.* He could walk away from a few hot kisses and a one-time love-making.

Then her tongue stroked his and raw male desire sent all his great plans, logical thinking and good in-tentions up in smoke.

His heart pounded, passion exploded and a raven-ous groan that had been eating at him for two days escaped his lips. He slid his hands under her sweat-shirt, needing to feel the warmth of her silken skin against his palms. He splayed his hand across her back.

He wanted more of her, unobstructed access. He pulled up her sweatshirt, revealing midriff, ribs, her plain white bra. ''So practical, so Charity.''

''I'm working on the practical part.''

He slipped the shirt over her head and tossed it free, watching it land on Misty's head. He unsnapped her bra and sent it airborne, to wind up across Misty's back. Charity drew in a quick hot breath, her passion almost palatable. She gasped, ''Maybe practical isn't so bad, after all.''

He grinned and fondled her breasts as they swelled, the nipples pinking. "Is that good for you?"

Her eyes darkened, her cheeks flushed. "Yes," she whispered. "Is it good for you?"

"Honey, if it was any better we'd both melt onto the floor." He kissed her. "And it's going to get a hell of a lot better."

She panted, "Don't know if I can stand better."

He winked, laughed wickedly and scooped her into his arms. Gently he laid her into the mound of clean, fresh hay, which gave way as she settled into it. Then he lay beside her and greedily took her left nipple deep into his mouth.

CHARITY FELT HER HEAD spin as he sucked at her other nipple, sending electric currents of desire racing through her.

"Not that I'm all that knowledgeable on the subject," she gasped. "But making love can't get better than this."

He looked at her, his eyes as dark as wet earth in the spring. He winked, then unsnapped her jeans and rested his hot hand possessively at the junction of her legs.

Barely controlled lust pulled his features into hard lines and Charity reveled in the fact that she had triggered it. If this was just sex to him and nothing more, then she'd have to deal with it...later. She unsnapped his jeans and slid down the zipper, feeling his erection surge against her fingers.

"We should take to going barefoot." He uttered a colorful expletive, sat back and yanked his boots off. He pulled off his shirt, spread it out on the hay and rolled her back onto it. Slowly, deliberately, tantalizingly, he slid off her jeans, flipped them aside and planted feather-light kisses at her navel...then below.

He parted her legs; her heart racing, her fingers traveled his dark, thick hair. His warm, moist lips connected with the inside of one thigh, then the other, filling her with never-felt-before ecstasy. "Tanner."

Was that her voice? She hoped so. She'd hate like heck for anyone else to be around. He slid off his jeans, located the condom and made himself ready for her.

He looked at her, his breathing uneven, fire in his eyes. Had there ever been a more perfect male specimen than Tanner Davenport—broad-shouldered, narrow-hipped, muscled legs and an erection that made her eyes widen? "Were...were you that big before?"

He flashed a lopsided grin. "You sure know how to flatter a guy, Kentucky Girl."

Then he lowered himself over her and she quivered in anticipation. Her legs parted more, her body welcoming his, as she fell back against the soft hay. His male heat encouraged her to open her legs wider still and he slowly pushed himself into her damp softness, filling every inch of her body and soul with his own.

She moaned and he kissed her as he pushed deeper still, as her hips arched to meet his. Then he moved, easily at first, driving her crazy with wanting, building a steady rhythm. Her entire body sizzled. Every nerve, every one of her senses was consumed by him. He took her higher and higher till she yelled his name, and they climaxed together, one in body and spirit and desire.

He kissed her hair, then nuzzled her neck as his body sagged onto hers, pushing her into the hay. If she could only stop time and keep Tanner with her, always like this. But that was impossible; he didn't care for her, at least not in a just-you-and-me-babe way. Being with him now was just another episode of *Great Sex* brought to you by Tanner Davenport. Dang. She couldn't blame him, only herself. He'd been perfectly honest with her.

Slowly he rolled from her to lie on his back, spread-eagled. "I think I've died and gone to heaven."

Every bone in Charity's body felt like Jell-O. "More heavenly than last time?"

"I think it's a tie. I wonder where our clothes are?"

She glanced around and giggled. "On the clothes-horse."

He cut his eyes her way and she nodded to Misty who was bedecked in her sweatshirt, pants and bra. Tanner laughed. "Hell of a way to treat a pregnant female."

"I'll give her extra oats. You know," she said, snuggling up to Tanner, loving the way his arm tugged her near, "you're a hero around here. If it wasn't for you and your iron bird it would have taken a lot longer to narrow down the problem on the Ridge and we could have lost horses."

"I was lucky." He kissed her forehead. "The scientists in Lexington and Patience and Mama Kay are the ones who pulled it all together."

"Yeah, but without you there wouldn't have been anything to pull. Your daddy would have been proud." She felt him stiffen at the mention of his father, but pressed on. It was important that he know what she knew. "Everybody cares what their parents think of them." She turned onto her side and kissed Tanner's cheek. "That's from your dad. He reminisced about you a lot. When I was working over at Thistledown, he'd come into the barn, talk to the horses, hum a few bars of 'My Old Kentucky Home' and—"

"*That's* what you were humming when I walked in tonight."

She smiled. "He taught me so many things. We'd discuss the horses, and you and Nathan and your mom and the good times you all had. Mostly he'd talk and I'd groom. I think he helped me to make up for losing you. He made a mistake and was too proud to admit it. I was his penance, Tanner."

She smiled. "Do you realize the one thing you both

have in common—besides a hard head, a dimpled chin and loving Nate—is helping me?''

Tanner let go of her and stood. He dusted off the hay, then wrestled on his briefs and jeans. He was quiet, too quiet. She sat.

''I know you're trying to help, Charity, but what happened between Dad and me happened a long time ago and nothing's going to undo it.''

She took her clothes for Misty and shrugged into her sweatshirt as Tanner retrieved his shirt from the hay pile. ''But maybe you can understand him a little better. He loved Thistledown and couldn't fathom why anyone wouldn't, especially his own son.''

''If he was alive I probably wouldn't have come home.''

''But you did come, to save Nate. And lo' and behold, you fit in fine around here.''

He pulled on his boots and slid her a sideways glance as she yanked on her jeans. ''So far I haven't saved Nate from anything. And as long as there was a need for me and my plane, I fit in. But now it's over.'' He smoothed back his tousled hair. ''Especially between us.''

She studied him, letting his words sink in. ''That's very interesting since I didn't realize there was anything between us in the first place. So tell me, *what's* over?''

His eyes rounded a fraction into an uh-oh expression and he sucked in a quick, guilty breath.

"You said this was all just sex between us. Some pretty great sex but nothing more. Right?"

"Right."

He started to walk away, but she snagged his arm, turning him back. He peered at her as his breath fell over her in a warm caress. "You're lying like a cheap rug, Tanner Davenport. You *do* care about me, just as Savannah said. And I know I care about you."

He squared his shoulders. "I'm not lying." Then his shoulders sagged an inch and his eyes narrowed. "How do you know I'm lying? And you really care about me?"

"Of course not. I just strip naked and jump into the hay with any man who waltzes in here. Ask Puck. Day and night, men stream in and out." She waved her arm around. "This isn't really a foaling barn, it's Charity's house of ill repute."

"I get the picture."

"And I know you're lying when you do that little half-smile thing. You did it when we were lost in that rainstorm when you said you knew where the cabin was."

"I *did* know."

She arched her brow.

"Look, it doesn't matter two hoots in a holler how much I care about you. You're here with the horses. I'm in Alaska with a partner and a business of my own, and that makes us as far apart as two people can get."

Chapter Ten

Charity looked at Tanner. "You care? About me?"

This was great, terrific, incredible. It was also the land of living hell. "But you're right. I can't exactly see myself trading in my horses for a dogsled team, and you already left the Ridge once because it didn't suit you. So now what?"

"Now nothing. That's the whole point."

She'd never considered Tanner as *nothing,* not after making love to him twice. "You want to forget *this* ever happened?" She kicked a clump of scattered hay back into the pile where they'd made love. "My memory isn't that bad, Tanner."

"Then we'll live with what happened between us and we won't let it happen again."

"What…what if it does?"

He framed her face with his hands and his eyes turned smoky. He traced her top lip with his thumb and brushed his lips across her forehead. He gazed into her eyes and said, "I might get back here once a year and the odds of you coming to Alaska are slim to none. What kind of relationship is that? It will be hard enough to walk away from whatever's going on between us right now without making it more complicated.''

''I'm a complication?''

He gave her a lopsided grin. ''Among other things, like gorgeous and provocative and sexy as hell. We'll keep our distance, let things cool off.''

Cool? Did he say cool? He had just recited the list of attributes every woman wants to hear from a man and now he wanted her to cool off? Ha! Then again, she didn't need to keep stoking this fire between them, either. ''Well, I guess that will work. But what about us breaking up this wedding? We still have five days.''

Tanner could cause a whole lot of problems in five days if she wasn't around to foil them.

''You haven't exactly provided a wealth of ideas on that score.''

''I've been thinking.''

''That's what you said before. We can meet up tomorrow night in town to talk over some ideas. Nate said there's going to be a little street party to celebrate. Most of the horses are on the mend and you can hear the hum of chainsaws taking down cherry tress everywhere. With so many people in town, we won't be tempted to get *complicated* there, that's for sure.''

Maybe keeping their distance would cool this *complication* between them. "Okay. In town tomorrow evening, at the Finish Line. Beer and pizza sound good."

She watched him walk off, thinking how rotten it would be when she saw him walk off for the last time to fly away in his silver bird. She loved the horses, the farm and the racing but at this moment, and only for a second, a part of her wished she'd sold the place and lived in town. Then she could go to Alaska to see just how complicated she and Tanner could get given half a chance. As it was, it looked as if they'd never get a chance.

LATE THE NEXT DAY Tanner parallel parked the truck on Main Street. It was great to see everyone out enjoying themselves, laughing, having a few hours of fun and not wringing their hands over sick horses. Not that all the horses had been instantly cured, but they were on their way and no new cases of illness had been reported. Life was good.

'Course when he'd meet up with Charity at the Finish Line, life would be great, even if they only met for a few minutes to discuss strategy for putting an end to Nate and Savannah's engagement. Being with Charity made everything more fun, more exciting, and he really looked forward to it. He'd have to remember these good times because they'd come to an end soon enough…as soon as he figured out how to break up Nate and Savannah.

He stopped to talk to two horse owners. They thanked him for delivering Mama Kay's yeast brew. Then two more owners joined in. Tanner was astounded and appreciative. Not because he enjoyed the praise so much, but because he was being accepted for who he was…a pilot. Charity was right, he did care what his dad thought and he bet his dad would have been proud.

Tanner smiled to himself, then realized he was smiling on the outside, too. It was the first time in a very, very long time that he'd smiled over anything associated with his dad.

He headed for the Finish Line and passed Payne's Drugstore, where the high school kids met to have sodas and to get a date for Saturday nights. Next was Togs for Tots, where mothers wrestled with their little ones to try on new spring clothes, and then Lilly's Lingerie. He spotted Savannah inside holding a long, flowing, sheer nightgown…though it probably had a more sophisticated name than *nightgown.*

She eyed him, then tapped on the window, beckoning him inside. He smiled politely and shook his head, declining her invitation. But before he'd taken two more steps down the sidewalk, she was out the door, standing beside him, linking her arm around his waist. She looked up at him and smiled sweetly. "I need your help."

He eyed at the frilly storefront of white lace and pink bows and held up his hands in protest. "No way. This stuff is way, way out of my league, worse than the perfume shop. I think you can make this kind of decision on your own."

"Help is always good, Tanner. You help me, I help you."

"What's that mean?"

She giggled and her arm seemed glued to his as she tugged him inside. He could either go with her or cause a scene because Savannah sure wasn't letting go.

The shop was filled with lacy panties, sheer, silky bras, slips and a lot of other things he'd seen but didn't know the proper names for. They were in every color imaginable and some unimaginable.

"I should leave. Remember what happened in the perfume store. I nearly passed out."

Savannah smiled wickedly and chuckled. "I *know* what happened at the perfume store and it had nothing to do with perfume."

"Sure it did."

She chuckled again. What did it mean? A chuckle like that always meant something was going on that he didn't know about but should. He hated that kind of chuckle.

"Savannah, can't we just meet up later?"

"You already have a date tonight, remember?"

She grinned and nodded at the next room, to Charity, as she studied a display of pink, white and red panties…if something so skimpy, so transparent, so soft and shimmering could be called panties. What happened to those white things she wore? Tanner wondered. Wisps of material that were probably bras of some sort in deep forest green and black were draped over her arms.

He stopped dead. He looked from the lingerie in her arms—to her lovely body that would be so damn provocative in such skimpy garments—to the display. He could imagine Charity in every one of those sexy little numbers.

His heart rate accelerated and a bead of pure male, testosterone-induced sweat slithered down his back. And he'd thought the perfume store and Ravish had driven him over the edge. They were nothing compared with see-through everything guaranteed to drive any man insane in one minute.

Hell, it had taken him less than a minute, and he'd only *imagined* Charity dressed in those lacy things. What would his reaction be if she actually *did* dress in them? He'd probably evaporate into a cloud of steam.

She glanced up, her gaze landing on him. Her jaw fell as her eyes bulged. "T-Tanner?"

"Hi?"

Savannah said, "Since you two were meeting up later, I thought I'd get Tanner in here now, so you wouldn't miss each other."

Charity regained her composure before he did and said to Savannah, "You brought him in *here?* A lingerie shop isn't exactly a hot meeting spot, you know."

Savannah shrugged. "Maybe not." She looked from one to the other. "Or maybe it is. Anyway, I want Tanner to take you out of here because your conservative ideas are giving me a headache." She snatched up a pair of white satin panties with pink bows that were more air than there. She said to Tanner, "These are her idea of what I should buy for my honeymoon. They would look great on her, don't you think? But they're not me."

Charity glanced around. "*Tanner!* This is not the Finish Line."

Yes it was. He was finished. Charity surrounded by all this sexy stuff would be impossible to forget. She glanced at the articles in her arms and turned three shades of red. "They're for Savannah," she said defensively.

Savannah pursed her lips. "They are not. You picked them out for yourself, said you were tired of that white stuff. I'm more an animal-print girl myself. Zebra for Mondays, leopard on Tuesdays, alligator on Wednesday." She nodded at a peignoir set draped over a royal-blue velvet chair. "And you picked that out, too."

"For you."

Savannah huffed. "I look awful in moss green. It's

you. Goes great with your hair. I'm going for the big pink boa and the black bustier I saw in the back. And there's a cute little French maid's outfit that should light Nate's fire."

Tanner shook his head, trying to make sense of all this. "French maid? For Nate? What about making an outfit out of the *Wall Street Journal*. Nate really likes the *Wall Street Journal*."

Savannah kissed Tanner's cheek. "Nathan is into much more than the *Journal* these days."

Charity dropped the bras and panties on the counter and snagged Tanner's arm. "We should go."

Savannah picked up the items Charity had dropped and handed them to the saleslady along with a credit card. "I'll bring these home for you. Didn't you say you burned all your old stuff?" She shrugged and grinned. "Hope you didn't burn *all* of it because what would you ever have on now?"

She winked at Tanner as Charity propelled him out of the shop, nearly pushing him down the stone steps. In a second they were outside on the sidewalk. She nodded across the street and pointed. "*That's* the Finish Line, remember?"

"Were those things in that store really for you?"

"Well…yes. Sort of. I was in there—" she nodded at the lingerie store "—to help Savannah pick out new things for her honeymoon and then…well… guess I got carried away." She shrugged. "Told you I was working on that *practical* thing."

If he didn't get his mind on something besides Charity in that sexy underwear, he'd make a spectacle of himself right in the middle of Main Street. Food was his only hope. He took her hand and headed for the Finish Line. "We'll need two pizzas."

"You must be starved. Aren't you afraid of getting…fat?"

"Got other things on my mind right now." *Like you!* He held open the door for Charity and followed her inside to a little table by the window. He buried his head behind the menu, pulled in a steadying breath and thought of pizza instead of Charity in sexy underwear.

She plucked the menu from his hand, turned it right-side up and put it back. "Are you all right?"

He put down the menu. "No. Are you?"

"Me?" She licked her lips and her eyes went dreamy. It took every ounce of Tanner's self-control to keep from diving across the table and taking her in his arms. Then she stiffened her spine and picked up the menu. "Let's order pizza."

"Yeah, pizza. And talk about how to break up the wedding." He looked around, trying to think of something besides Charity. "I like the candles in the wine bottles and red-checked tablecloths. Nice touch."

"The place was remodeled last year, even has a party room out back."

He slapped his hand on the table. "That's it, a party. I'll throw Nate a bachelor party, in the party room after the rehearsal dinner tomorrow night."

"What are you talking about? Why would you do that?"

He sat back and gave her an easy smile, then asked a question he already knew the answer to. "Tell me, did you happen to come up with some wonderful idea to break up Nathan and Savannah apart? Helping Savannah pick out a French maid outfit and a bustier—whatever the hell that is—isn't the way to end an engagement, is it?" He raised an accusing brow.

"Those were Savannah's ideas."

"I don't think your heart is in this, so I'm going to throw Nathan the bachelor party of all bachelor parties. Get some cute girls to host it. Show Nate what he'll be missing when he takes himself off the market to marry Savannah. Bachelor parties are always good for leading men astray."

Her eyes widened by half. "They are?"

"Absolutely. Last one I went to in Anchorage, this amazingly beautiful woman popped out of a cake and the soon-to-be groom called off the wedding right on the spot."

This was better, got his mind off Charity…except for that soft pink blouse she wore that fit her lovely shape perfectly, and the way her eyes sparkled in the candlelight. "I can get a dancing girl to come up from

Lexington to do one of her little teaser numbers for Nate and—''

''A *stripper?*'' She hadn't screeched that loud since the caterpillar incident in the pasture. Half the people in the diner turned her way.

He sat up. ''Not exactly a stripper, but close, and—''

''No way. Out of the question. Impossible. Bad idea. No strippers.''

''Why not?''

''Because...because...'' She nibbled her lower lip. ''What about going to a movie? Bet Nate hasn't been to a movie in a long time. Bet he'd like that.''

''And how's that supposed to keep him from marrying Savannah?''

''Go see some shoot-'em-up thing. Something with deNiro or Willis. Savannah hates them. He'll see how mismatched he and Savannah are and—''

He rested his elbows on the table and leaned toward her, catching a whiff of...*Ravish?* From the perfume shop? How was he supposed to think about a bachelor party and girls popping out of cakes with Charity wearing Ravish...especially when that's exactly what he'd like to do to her. Damnation!

He looked at Charity, focusing on the party. He swallowed and ran his hand over his face. ''The bachelor party is the answer. After the rehearsal dinner. You throw Savannah a bachelorette party, have punch and cookies and watch *When Harry Met Sally*. She won't suspect a thing."

Charity's eyes brightened. Too bright. She gave him a saucy grin. Oh, hell, now what? She wasn't smiling like that for kicks.

"Well now, Mr. Davenport, that's a great idea you have there."

"It is?" Why did he suddenly know it was a really bad idea?

"I can get some of those Chip-n-dales to come entertain us and—"

"Chip-n-dales?"

She grinned hugely. "One of the girls I graduated from high school with has a brother who does a routine like that for parties. Bet I can get him on short notice. We'll have a great time. Those guys are so cute, and so well built, yummy, and have the nicest buns and—"

"Yummy? What's with this yummy stuff? Where'd that come from? No, no, no. Punch and cookies is all you'll need."

"That's not all *you* need."

He spread his arms wide. "I'm breaking up the engagement. This is just…business."

"Wonder how many guys have used that line."

"It's to distract Nate and what difference does it make to you if I have party girls or not?"

She stood and smiled sweetly. "It doesn't. I think the parties are a fine idea. You…and your guests watch scantily clad women shaking their wares and I get to do the same with the men.''

'''*I?*'''

''And my guests,'' she added quickly, but not quickly enough. She snapped around, her hair flying in the air like red silk ribbons as he watched her sashay her way across the floor, her hips swaying just enough to drive any man out of his mind. When had she started doing that? And he wasn't the only one noticing. Two guys at the corner table arched their brows in her direction.

Hellfire! She was going to enjoy this Chip-n-Dale idea. The last thing he wanted was Charity MacKay ogling another man. He gave the guys in the corner a beady-eyed stare. He sure as hell didn't want another man to be ogling her!

CHARITY SAT at the kitchen table, drumming her fingers against the wood top as Mama and Savannah addressed seating cards.

''The rehearsal dinner went well,'' Mama said.

''Peachy.'' Except all Charity could think about was the bachelor party afterward. The last thing Charity wanted was for Tanner Davenport to be eyeing another woman…or another woman to be eyeing him. The fact that he was heading back to Alaska didn't matter. This was now.

She drummed harder till Savannah reached over, flattening Charity's hand with her own. ''Enough, already. If you don't stop, you're going to drive me and Mama and Patience here plumb crazy. So, Tanner and Nate are at a bachelor party tonight, so what.''

"And Puck," Mama added in a tight voice as she folded another place card, not sounding all that thrilled about the party, either.

Savannah picked up another card and folded it. "How bad can it be?"

Patience shrugged as she studied from some big thick book with little print. "Men have been going to bachelor parties forever. It's a right of passage passed down through the ages from generation to—"

"Can it, Patience," Charity growled.

Patience huffed, "I can't imagine what the big deal is?"

That's because Patience wasn't the one who was wild about Tanner and half crazy with jealousy. Charity froze. Was she jealous? *Heck, yes.* That was one of the reasons she hated this party idea. The second reason she hated it was that Savannah's wedding could possibly end up being no wedding. *Shouldn't that be the first reason?*

She looked at Savannah's sparkling-white, silk-and-satin wedding dress hanging from the hall light fixture so as not to touch the floor or get mussed in some closet. She looked at the peach dresses hanging in the doorway that she and Patience would wear, *if* this wedding came off and Tanner Davenport didn't louse up the whole thing. "This isn't just any old bachelor party."

Savannah arched her perfect brow. "What do you mean?"

Oh, boy, she shouldn't have said that. She didn't want Savannah to know Tanner was trying to stop her marrying Nathan, because if the wedding did come off there'd be hard feelings. Charity didn't want there to be hard feelings. "Nothing. Not really. Just a few hostesses at the Finish Line."

Patience flipped a page in her book. "Doesn't sound normal to me. Thought there'd be strippers or something."

Charity glared. "And how would *you* know about such things, baby sister?"

"Common knowledge. Men don't go to bachelor parties to knit. And I am no baby in spite of what you-all think."

Charity stood. "It's not going to be like that." She smiled reassuringly at Savannah. "Everything will be fine. We could have gone to Lexington to see the Chip-n-Dales, but none of you seemed interested."

Patience slid off the bar stool and grinned like a cat who'd just discovered cheese. "Speak for yourself. I was interested, plenty interested. You are just a bunch of stick-in-the-muds."

Charity paced from one end of the kitchen to the other. She wrung her hands and swiped perspiration from her brow. What if Tanner was successful and

Nathan did call off the wedding? It wouldn't be because he didn't love Savannah; it would be because Tanner was sticking his Alaskan nose where it didn't belong. She paced faster and wrung her hands again until Savannah stood in front of her, stopping Charity midstep.

She gave Charity a hard look. "What in the world is wrong with you? You said there was nothing going on at this bachelor party but you're fretting about like some caged lion. What's going on?"

"Nothing."

She put her hands on her hips. "Spill it, Charity. I know you and you're a terrible liar."

Actually, she'd been getting better at it.

Mama said to Charity, "If Tanner's still up to what I think he's up to, you should tell Savannah. It is her life, her marriage."

Savannah's eyes rounded to the size of golf balls. "Okay, that's it. What's Tanner going to do? I have a right to know if everyone else does."

Charity sucked in a deep breath. She didn't want to rat out Tanner, but she'd had no success in squelching his stupid quest to break up the engagement. Time to call in reinforcements.

She turned to Savannah. "Tanner thinks you and Nathan aren't a good match. That Nathan's just besotted with you and hasn't really thought about what he's doing and he needs to experience more women before jumping into marriage. And that you'll get bored with Nathan in no time and be off to L.A. or—"

"I'll kill Tanner Davenport with my bare hands!" Savannah snatched Patience's book off her lap. "I'll beat him to a pulp with—" she read the spine "—*Life History of the Arachnid* for interfering in my life. I'll make him wish he *was* an arachnid. I thought we were friends!"

"You are. That's the trouble. He thinks you're too much like him to be a good match for Nathan." Charity took the book from Savannah. "Calm down. There's nothing to say that the strippers and near-naked women jumping out of cakes will sway Nathan or even tempt him and—"

"What?" Savannah snagged the book from Charity. "There are naked women at this…this *party?*"

Charity shrugged. "I don't know if they're *all-the-way* naked or just a little naked."

"Where's another book?" Savannah scanned the room. "This is a two-book job."

Mama stood and smoothed back her perfect hair. "Well, I can't speak for the rest of you, but I don't like my man peering at other woman."

Charity exchanged looks with Patience and Savannah. Together they said, *"My* man?"

Mama looked unruffled. "I think it's time the MacKay women put an end to this little party."

Savannah charged for the front door with Mama behind her. Patience turned to Charity. "We better go. When Savannah finds Tanner there will be bloodshed. We might have to save him.''

Charity shrugged and winked at Patience. ''Or not. Tanner Davenport got himself into this. He can darn well reap the rewards.''

Chapter Eleven

Charity pulled the old station wagon around the side of the Finish Line to the back party room. She, Patience, Mama and Savannah, still toting the bug book, got out. Mama said, "Well, the music's sure loud enough. They're all going to be deaf as stones before the night's over." She went up on the porch, cupped her hands together at the window and peeked inside. "It's packed in there. Some shindig."

Savannah looked in the next window. "I see Sally Baine prancing around shaking her wares. Always wondered if everything she had was real."

Charity put her face to the window. "Guess what, it's real, all right. Don't see Nathan or Tanner or Puck. Isn't that Sheriff Woods in a hula skirt doing the limbo? And Patience standing on a table?"

Charity took her face from the window and looked around. "How the heck did Patience get in there so fast?"

Mama and Savannah pulled back from the windows they'd been peering through and heard Patience suddenly yell over the din, ''Heads up. Anybody seen Tanner Davenport?''

Sally yelled back, ''He and Nathan and Puck left. Said we could all stay because everything was paid for.'' Sally jumped up on a table and did a shimmy and laughed. ''They sure are missing one heck of a party.''

Patience slid from the table and joined the rest of the MacKay clan outside. ''Guess you heard. So, now what? The Three Musketeers aren't here?''

Charity growled, ''Or maybe they just took select female guests and moved the party somewhere else.''

Savannah scowled. ''Somewhere more private. Let's go ask in the diner. Maybe someone saw the scalawags take off and knows where they're headed.''

She led the way to the main entrance of the Finish Line. As they entered, she stopped in the doorway and pointed, arm extended to the bar. ''There they are.''

Nate, Tanner and Puck sat on bar stools, their backs to the entrance—blue Oxford shirt, flannel shirt, denim shirt. Perfectly neat haircut, needed a haircut, not much hair to cut. The three of them were drinking beer and watching a basketball game on the TV over the bar.

''Tanner Davenport,'' Charity yelled over the din.

''You no-good rotten scoundrel,'' Savannah added as she tossed her hair. ''What do you think you're doing trying to break up my wedding and lead my fiancé astray.''

The diner was filled with patrons and every one of them went dead quiet as the three men turned and faced the three women. The patrons stared. Tanner opened his mouth, then shut it. "Uh…"

Charity went up to the stool he was sitting on and brought her face to within an inch of his. "Where are the hootchie-cootchie girls you hired to woo Nathan?"

Tanner shrugged. "There aren't any girls."

"Like heck. You said you were going to get girls, show Nathan a good time and break up his engagement. So where are they, huh? Where do you have them stashed? Some hotel room for after-the-game fun for you and Nathan and Puck?"

Before Tanner replied, Nathan asked, "What's this about breaking up our wedding? That's crazy. Tanner wouldn't do that." He looked Tanner in the eye. "Would you?"

TANNER STROKED HIS JAW. He was obviously not Mr. Wonderful in anyone's book right now. He said to Charity in a stage whisper, "Thought you were behind me on this? Thought we were partners."

She gave him a slitty-eyed look. "I was just pretending. So I could find out what you were up to and try to stop you before you succeeded."

His eyes opened wide. "You lied?"

"Maybe a little. White lies, to save Savannah's marriage."

"That's the way these MacKay girls are," came Billy Ray's voice from across the room. He glanced down at his brother and smirked. "Those women stick together like glue. 'Course you can keep Savannah there in line by showing her the back of your hand once in a while."

Nathan spun around and faced Billy Ray. "You hurt *my* Savannah?"

Tanner caught a flash of angry fire in Nate's eyes before his brother lunged across the room, grabbed Billy by the shirt and decked him, sending him ass-over-appetite across the table. *Dang, didn't know Nate had it in him.* Tanner came up behind Nate—backup was always a good idea in these situations—until Nate ducked and Billy Ray's fist connected with Tanner's jaw, landing him on the floor.

Well, hell. How'd that happen? Little stars danced in front of his eyes for a second; then he saw Puck come over as Silas Ray came up beside Billy. Tanner scrambled to his feet. Big-and-ugly Silas would make mincemeat out of the lean Puck. But one of Nate's barn managers blocked a punch aimed for Puck and Tanner connected his fist to Silas's jaw. Payback time.

In the blink of an eye—probably a black eye— Tanner saw another of Nate's barn hands take on one of Billy Ray's supporters. Charity dumped a pitcher of beer over Silas's head followed by a basket of peanut shells, and half the diner erupted into punching and ducking. Chairs and tables crashed to the floor; wine bottles, beer bottles and pizza flew everywhere.

Tanner turned around in time to see Savannah stand on a chair and crack Billy Ray over the head with the biggest book in the county. Where'd that come from? Tanner wondered. Billy turned, glared at Savannah, then his eyes rolled around like BBs in a box and he fell to the floor in a crumpled heap.

Never before had Tanner seen Savannah look so pleased with herself, or Nate so concerned…even when his horses were sick. Nate snatched Savannah from the chair and flattened her against the wall, protecting her from the mayhem. *Dang, was she Frenching him in the ear?*

Tanner felt a jab to his ribs and dodged another punch. He better start paying attention to the fighting or he'd get killed.

Sheriff Woods suddenly yelled, "All right, break it up!"

He stood on a chair and yanked off his hula skirt. "Can't a man do a little partying without all hell breaking loose? *Dagnabbit.*"

He looked at the men and the mess in the corner. "Who threw the first punch that got this going?"

"That would be me," Nathan called, still standing in front of Savannah.

"You?" Sheriff Woods's mouth flapped open and shut a few times before he said, "Well, I'll be."

"But he was defending me." Savannah beamed as she waved at Sheriff Woods. She kissed Nathan on the cheek. "So I'm the guilty one."

"Actually," Tanner said, "it's my fault because I got Nate in here in the first place."

"And me," Charity chimed in. "If I had just told Savannah what was going on with Tanner and his stupid idea in the first place, none of us would be here and—"

"Enough," roared the sheriff. He glanced down at Billy Ray still crumpled on the floor. "What happened to him?"

Savannah shrugged. "The arachnids got him."

Sheriff Woods raked his hair and shook his head. "I have no idea what's going on here. Nathan, you're coming with me. My deputy's getting the rest of your names and you're all splitting the cost to put the Finish Line back together."

"No need," Nathan said. "I'll pay for it." He eyed the blob on the floor, walked over and nudged the butt portion with the toe of his tasseled loafer. "With pleasure I'll pay for it." He turned to Savannah, tipped her back across his arm and gave her a kiss right out of some forties movie. The whole diner erupted in applause and wolf whistles.

Tanner followed Nathan-the-hero and Savannah and Sheriff Woods out to the cruiser and watched as

Nathan got locked into the back seat. Never had he expected to see his even-tempered, dress-shirted, crease-panted brother being hauled off in the sheriff's cruiser. Hell, that was Tanner's role. Least, it had been.

Savannah turned to Tanner. "What are we going to do? We can't let Nathan rot in jail."

"I don't think he'll rot in one night, but I'll take care of it." He stiffened in chagrin. "Look, this is my fault. I'm sorry, Savannah, I really am. You and Nathan are clearly in love. I've made a mess of things for both of you."

Savannah smiled. "Yeah, you did. But I got to whack Billy Ray. I've wanted to do that longer than you can imagine." She kissed Tanner. "You're forgiven."

He gritted his teeth. "That's incredibly kind of you. But I doubt my brother is going to let me off the hook so easily."

Savannah laughed. "Guess that's between you and Nathan." She winked. "Why did you and Nathan and Puck leave the party around back?"

"Well, Nathan's only interested in one girl, with or without clothes on. *You.* All Puck could talk about was the great time he and Mama Kay had in Lexington."

"And you?"

He shrugged. "I don't know. Follow the crowd, I guess."

"*You* follow the crowd? That'll be the day." She tipped her chin, looking very wise. "You didn't stay at the party with all those girls because they don't interest you. You're in love with Charity. Now you just have to decide what in blazes you're going to do about it."

Tanner watched Savannah strut her stuff back into the Finish Line. Then he headed for the sheriff's office. Savannah was wrong. He didn't love Charity. He *liked* her, liked her a lot, but none of this love stuff for him. Not that it mattered, because as soon as this wedding was over he was out of here. He had a business to run in Alaska. His partner was counting on him. May was a busy time, the ice was melting and tourists and businessmen would be heading north.

But he could think about all this later. First he had to bail Nate out of the pokey and himself out of hot water. He hoped Nate was in a forgiving mood because he packed a pretty mean left hook when he was mad. Who would have thought?

Tanner wrote Sheriff Woods a check for Nate's bail and a check to cover the damages at the Finish Line. Then he sat on the wooden bench in the hallway and waited for his brother. This was a new experience: Nate had always been the one waiting for him.

When Nate finally arrived, Tanner stood. "If you want to punch my lights out hold off till we get home. You don't need to get arrested twice in one night."

Nathan grinned, opening up a cut in his lower lip.

He dabbed it with his shirtsleeve, leaving red marks on the blue Oxford. "Hell, you just thought you were helping me even if your idea was stupid. Nothing you could do would keep me from marrying Savannah. We're in love, will be forever, and that's not going to change for anything or any one. Besides—" his expression turned serious "—it gave me a chance to deck Billy Ray. I had no idea he'd mistreated her like that."

"Savannah did pretty good herself."

Nate nodded and winked. "That's my girl."

"You're good for each other. Bring out the best." Tanner studied Nate for a moment. His brother was different, more relaxed, happier, centered, very much a man in love. How could he have missed it? Because he was a hardhead and thought he had all the answers, that's how.

He said, "I already apologized to Savannah and we're okay, though when she realizes her handsome groom will have double shiners for their wedding she may change her mind."

"What about Charity?" Nate asked. "Are things square between you two? I thought she was going to wring your neck."

Tanner grinned. "Yeah, Charity's going to be a problem. You and Savannah are operating under the influence of love. Charity's not."

Nate chuckled and slapped Tanner on the back as they left the building. Dang it all, it was *that* chuckle again, the same one Savannah had given him at the lingerie shop. The one that said something was going on and everyone knew it except him. So, what was it he was missing?

TANNER CHECKED for the rings in the breast pocket of his tux for the millionth time, then knocked on Nate's bedroom door and went in. "Almost ready, Wedding Boy?"

Nate turned from the mirror and held out his hands. "The tux, shoes, shirt are fine, but there's no fixing the yellow-and-purple eyes."

"Think of it as a fashion statement. You'll match the flowers."

Nate laughed. "These wedding pictures are going to be a hit for a long time to come. Can you imagine trying to explain them to our kids?"

"Kids?"

"Two, three…dozen or so."

Tanner laughed, then pulled an envelope from his pocket. He handed it to Nate. "Airline tickets to Alaska. For you and Savannah." He rested his hand on Nate's shoulder. Tanner's chest suddenly tightened like steel bands on a wood barrel, and his voice sounded hoarse as he said, "I don't want it to be another seven years before we see each other again."

"It doesn't have to be this way, little brother. You could stay. We can share a jail cell next time Billy Ray gets out of line. Thistledown is half yours. All you have to do is say the word and you can move in here and—''

Tanner shook his head. ''Thistledown is yours. The house, the barns, the horses. That's the way Dad wanted it. I could never be happy here.'' He held up his hand to cut off Nate's protest. ''And that's okay. Dad and I never saw eye-to-eye on anything, except Charity MacKay. He helped her save her place and I respect him for that. Hell, I'm…grateful.''

''Have you ever wondered *why* you're so grateful?''

''Sure. Kept the best fried chicken a mile down the road.''

Nate gave him that know-it-all chuckle. ''There's more to it than that, but it's a start.''

''We better get going. If we're late Savannah will skin us alive.''

Nate exhaled a deep breath.

''Wedding jitters?''

He looked Tanner in the eyes. ''When Savannah and I get back from our honeymoon, you'll be gone.''

Tanner nodded at the tickets in his hand. ''Yeah, but I'm only a plane flight away. Alaska is God's country, you'll love it.''

''What I love is you, little brother.'' He tucked the tickets in his inside breast pocket and patted it as he said, ''Come August, Savannah and I will be on your doorstep. And you'll come here for Christmas?''

Tanner pulled in a deep breath. ''Yeah, Christmas.'' He took Nate in a bear hug. "I wish you all the happiness in the world, Nate.''

He grinned as he headed for the door. "Then you got your wish, because you're looking at the happiest man on earth.''

CHARITY SCURRIED INTO the kitchen and picked up the clipboard from the table. Flowers, *check*. Garter, *check*. Grandma's pearls, *check*.

Savannah swished into the kitchen. "Charity dressed, no check.''

Charity glanced up, ready to offer a perfectly good explanation as to why her dress was still upstairs and not on her body, but her words died in her throat. Love and joy filled her heart. "Oh, Savannah. You're so beautiful.''

Her dress shimmered in the late-afternoon sunlight, her skin glowed with happiness and her eyes sparkled. "No wonder they call the wedding day the bride's day.''

Savannah grinned. "It is a wonderful dress, isn't it?''

"It's not the dress, it's you.''

She scrunched up her cute nose. "It's Nate. Thinking of him makes me this way.''

Mama came into the room followed by Patience. Charity said to Patience, "You sure do clean up nice for a dirt digger.'' Then said to Mama, "The green suit is perfect.''

"Are you going to be maid of honor in your slip?" Patience asked.

"I'm working on it. Just give me a minute here. I'm a busy woman."

"You think nothing will happen unless you make it happen."

She shrugged. "That, too." She looked at her sisters, then at Mama and put down the clipboard and pulled in a deep breath. "We'll never be together like this again, just the four of us. Not that it's a bad thing, just—"

"Different," Savannah added in a soft voice.

"Yeah, different," Charity confirmed.

Mama said, "We've been there for each other all along, through tears and laughter. When no one else believed in us—" she took Savannah's hand, then Patience's and smiled at Charity "—we believed in each other. That's never going to change no matter where we go or who we marry."

Mama went to the cabinet and took down a box, opened it and dropped four gold rings in her palm. She gave one to Charity, one to Patience, one to Savannah and put one on her own pinky.

"They have a little bow on top," Patience noted.

Mama nodded. "Because we're tied together by love."

Patience's eyes welled as she slid on the ring.

"Don't you dare cry," Charity ordered. "This is a time of great happiness and joy, no tears today."

"I was just thinking—" she said as she turned to each of them "—that when I go back to school I wish I could rub the ring and you'd all just be there."

They exchanged looks, all wishing the very same thing. Then Mama said, "Well, we have a wedding to go to. Nathan'll be spitting mad if we don't get his bride to him on time."

Charity headed for the front door, but no one followed. "What's wrong?" She held up the clipboard. "Everything's checked off. We're ready. We did it, we really did it. It all worked out. Savannah's getting married."

Savannah grinned and kissed Charity's cheek. "Even if my big sister wears a slip, a smile and nothing else, I am, indeed, getting married today."

Chapter Twelve

Charity took her place as maid of honor and looked at Savannah and Nathan. As they exchanged rings and vows, white apple blossom petals floated in the air like fairy dust; the setting sun warmed the earth, and a sky swiped with pinks and purples formed the perfect canopy. Savannah and Nathan were pronounced husband and wife. They kissed and if angels parted the heavens and sang, *Hallelujah,* it wouldn't have surprised Charity one bit. *Cinderella, eat your heart out.*

"Well," Tanner said as he took Charity's arm and led her down the white cloth-covered aisle past hundreds of smiling guests. "They're married."

Charity kept a smile plastered on her own face but arched an accusing brow. "No thanks to you."

"Think again, Kentucky Girl. Keeping track of me gave *you* something to do for the last two weeks. You would have driven Savannah and Nate crazy with getting things organized. I can just see you running around with a clipboard.''

Her smile faulted. "Okay, who snitched?"

"You *really* had a clipboard?"

"Only a little one. And it helped with all the last-minute details." *Except for remembering to put on my own dress.*

She looked into his brown eyes and a heaviness settled in her heart knowing she wouldn't be seeing them much longer. "And now it's all over."

"Yeah. It's over." They stopped at the end of the aisle and he kissed her lightly on the lips, making her feel sad beyond words. They joined the receiving line, then posed for pictures and more pictures.

The sun set and there was food and champagne and dancing, and Tanner always seemed to be somewhere other than where she was. Mama came over to Charity as she sat by an ice sculpture of a galloping horse and asked, "Are you still mad at Tanner? You two aren't spending much time together."

"Savannah and Nathan didn't draw and quarter Tanner for trying to break them up, so I let him off the hook. Besides, I lied my head off to him, so I suppose we're even."

Across the lawn, now sporting lawn torches and a dance floor, a shapely blonde hung on Tanner's every word. "He sure seems to be having a jolly good time," Charity added through clenched teeth.

"He's probably saying goodbye to everyone since

he's leaving tomorrow. He helped a lot of people while he was here and they're not likely to forget it.''

"Tomorrow?'' Charity cut her eyes to Mama.

"He called his partner in Alaska. They just landed a big contract. Business is booming.'' Mama took her hand. "It may not be the best time to tell you this, dear, but I've put it off long as I dare since you were likely to become suspicious and wonder what was going on and—''

"The real reason Tanner has to get back is because he's married to an Eskimo beauty and has ten kids.''

"No, Puck and I got married. And why would you care if Tanner was married to an Eskimo beauty?''

She stared at Mama, then finally sputtered, "You…you and Puck? Married?''

Cheeks rosy, eyes sparkling, Mama said, "Got hitched in Lexington when we were there. It all kind of just happened this time. It seemed right.''

"This time?"

"He asked me before. Twice. I never thought I had anything to offer Puck but a messed-up life. Then I started getting involved with the horses and the farm and went to Lexington and helped the scientists and vets and…well, I feel better about myself than I have in a long time.'' She patted Charity's hand. "I can make him a good wife now. I didn't want to marry him until I could.''

Mama shook her head. "The caterpillars were a

near disaster for everyone except me. Funny how things work out. I couldn't be happier.''

"Neither could I.'' She hugged Mama tight. "Why didn't you tell us before now?''

"Didn't want to take away from Savannah and Nathan's big day. But I'm telling you now because…''

She turned red as an oak leaf in autumn and fidgeted. Mama never fidgeted. Good heavens, now what?

"You see,'' she continued. "Savannah will be on her honeymoon and Patience is spending the night at a friend's, and if Puck and I spend time together…night time together…well…'' Her blush deepened. "I thought you should know what was going on. We'll make a formal announcement next week.''

Night time? Mama and Puck? Who would have thought? "When Savannah and Nathan get back,'' Charity promised, "we'll have a party, invite everyone. This is wonderful news. You deserve this, Mama. You and Puck deserve each other.''

Mama kissed her on the cheek. "I'm so glad you approve.''

"Approve? I'm thrilled to pieces.''

She laughed. "I hope your sisters feel the same way. I'm off to tell Patience. Then I'll tell Savannah before she and Nathan leave.''

"Puck's been a part of our family since…forever. He just happened to live over the garage.'' Charity shrugged and grinned. "And now he won't.''

"Thank you, dear. Thank you for understanding. Then again, you always do." Her eyes misted. "No mother could be more proud of her daughter than I am of you, Charity. Savannah, Patience and I wouldn't have made it without your strength and drive. You're the one who pulled us through."

"We pulled each other."

"It was you, dear. I'll never forget that."

Charity's throat tightened and she looked at the gold ring with the bow on her little finger. "That's why you gave us these, isn't it?"

Mama grinned. "There are two more in our family now, but the four of us—the MacKay women—will always have a special bond."

She watched as Mama walked off. It was really more of a float, since Mama's feet never touched ground. Mama and Puck would be happy together just as Nathan and Savannah would be.

Charity suddenly felt incredibly alone. Mama's and Savannah's happiness made her realize that she'd never be happy like that because...because Tanner was leaving and she couldn't imagine caring for another man the way she cared for him.

Ah, poop. Who was she kidding? She didn't just *care* for Tanner, she was head-over-heels, mind-bogglingly ga-ga in love with the man, and there wasn't one blasted thing she could do except *get over it*. And how in Hades was she supposed to do that?

TANNER WATCHED the full moon as it hung in the west sky and lit the path that connected the MacKay farm to Thistledown. He found the Big Dipper, drew a line from the two end stars and homed in on the North Star. He'd done that very thing as a kid, lying in the fields at night, looking at the heavens and wondering what it would be like to be up there.

He could always tell where he was from that star. So why did he feel so lost now? He was going home, to Alaska, and should be happy as a lizard on a sunwashed rock.

He reached the end of the path and eyed the clapboard house, then the barn. Misty Kay was due to foal anytime and Charity MacKay would be there...probably with her clipboard. He smiled into the darkness, then headed for the foaling barn, a dim light visible through the window.

"Charity?" he whispered as he entered.

"Over here." She sat on a hay bale, flashlight beside her, knees to her chin. "What are you doing here at 2:00 a.m.?"

He sat next to her and nodded at the extra-large stall where Misty pawed at the hay. "It's closer to four. Think tonight's the night?"

"Trying to predict Mother Nature is tough, but just to be on the safe side I wrapped her tail and washed her down. All the signs are there. Calcium and magnesium levels are up, sporadic eating. She lay down once and I thought, *This is it,* then she got back up.

I've chewed every fingernail to the quick and ruined a very expensive manicure.''

''Are you expecting problems?''

She shook her head, her hair shining in the moonlight that filtered through the window. He shoved his hands into his pockets to keep from reaching out and touching it...just one more time.

''I don't want to leave anything to chance.''

''Is that why you left the reception early?''

She spread her hands, palms up in innocence. ''Hey, I was there to miss the bouquet.''

''You dodged it. Savannah tossed it right to you.''

''I slipped.''

She looked at him, starlight in her eyes, her lovely mouth soft and welcoming. But this was not the time for kissing. This was the time to say goodbye. ''Word has it you've got yourself a new stepdaddy.''

She nodded, smiling into the night. ''I knew Mama would tell you before you left.'' Her eyes darkened as they focused on him. ''When are you leaving?''

Her voice was low, sad, searing his heart. He shrugged because he suddenly couldn't get the words out. He cleared his throat. ''First light. My partner's swamped. I've left Grady in a mess taking off like I did, not that he'd ever complain. He's got some help, but it is my business, too.''

She touched his cheek and a shudder of pure ecstasy flowed through him.

''What's he like?''

"Grady? Built-in radar system, could find his way across Alaska blindfolded." He winked. "The perfect guy for Patience."

"Who gets lost on her own farm." Charity smiled. That was good, there wasn't much to smile about right now. Quiet surrounded them except for the soft whinny of the mares and the croaking of frogs down by the creek that flowed through both farms.

Tanner thought of the blue stone he kept in his pocket and how he'd grabbed it from there on impulse seven years ago when he'd left. He'd been in a hurry to leave then. Things were different this time. Way different.

Charity gasped and her eyes widened. She looked to Misty's stall and whispered, "She's down."

Tanner and Charity quietly made their way to the stall, staying outside, peering over the top. Tanner said, "Does she look okay?"

Charity held up her hand and crossed her fingers. Worry clouded her eyes and her jaw was clenched. He draped his arm around her, tugging her close. "Hang tight, Kentucky Girl. Misty's going to be a good mama."

They waited and watched.

"I wonder how long this will take."

Tanner checked his watch. "It's been ten minutes."

"Seems like ten years." She gripped his hand as the water bag appeared, then broke.

"So far, so good."

"There's a foot." Excitement charged her voice. "And another…and the nose and head. It has a star on its head." Tears slid down her cheeks as she held his hand in a death grip. The foal's back slid into view. Then there was a pause.

"Ohmigod."

"What?"

"The rest is taking too long. This isn't normal. Her hips are locked." Charity slipped into the stall and knelt beside Misty's head, stroking the mare. She said to Tanner, "You pull on the foal, and I'll keep Misty calm. I've got to keep her down. If she gets up, we'll have a disaster."

Tanner took one look at the foal's helpless face, fought off the urge to say, *I don't know anything about birthing horses* and got into the stall, hunkering down beside the foal. "What do you want me to do?"

"Gently pull the foal in a downward direction toward Misty's heels. That will relieve the lock."

Tanner felt his heart jump to warp speed as adrenaline and terror kicked in. *Damn*, why hadn't he paid attention when his father had tried to teach him? He would be much more help to Charity now if he hadn't been so stubborn then. Charity was right: he was a hardhead like his father and it had cost them both dearly.

Carefully, Tanner took hold of the foal, slippery little devil, and pulled. Somewhere in the back of his mind he offered a prayer that his father's sure hands would guide him now.

"That's it, not too hard, a little more…" And suddenly the foal slipped out, knocking Tanner off balance and landing flat on top of him. The foal looked down at him with the biggest brown eyes Tanner had ever seen.

"Don't move."

"What do you mean, don't move? I have a horse on top of me."

"It's only a little horse and the blood from the cord is flowing into the foal. Just stay still for a few more minutes. I have to keep Misty down for a while or she'll injure herself."

He oh, so gently stroked the foal's forehead and muzzle. "I think we're bonding."

"How does Tanner's Pride sound to you for his name?"

Tanner's heart tightened. This foal was Charity's hopes and dreams and more hard work had gone into bringing this little guy into the world than Tanner cared to think about. That she had named her foal after him touched him deeply. "I'm thinking Charity's Pride."

"Without you, this foal wouldn't have made it. Besides, when I start to train him it will be nice to say, 'Tanner do this' or 'Tanner do that,' and, wonder of wonders, he'll do it."

The foal suddenly found his legs, wobbled and

stood. Tanner sat up, amazement filling every inch of
him. This was what Charity and his dad and every
other horse farmer lived for. They were the protectors,
the caretakers of the horses, the land, and Tanner
hadn't really understood that till he'd seen it through
Charity eyes. She'd taken him by the hand and said,
*Look at this. It may not be your life, but it is won-
derful and you can appreciate it.* She never demanded
he be anything other than himself. He grabbed a towel
and rubbed the foal. "He's a beauty, Charity."

She beamed as she studied the foal. Another tear
slid down her cheek. "He's a contender, I just know
it. I can *feel* it." She wiped the tear. "And I owe you
new pants and shirt. You're a mess."

He stood as the foal teetered on long spindly legs.
The light outside hinted pearl-gray as Puck and Mama
strolled through the open doors into the barn.

"Well, I'll be darned," Puck whispered, looking
like a proud papa. Mama leaned over the stall. "Look
what we have here."

Tanner came to Charity and kissed her hair. Then
her gaze met his and a bone-numbing chill of deso-
lation more potent than anything he'd ever experienced in Alaska fell over him. "I'll be back at Christmas."

She forced a smile. "Christmas."

Things would be different then, and that was good
because saying goodbye was tearing his heart out.

Slowly, he turned and walked from the barn. What else could he do besides leave?

MORNING INCHED TO NOON as Charity tried to fight off the gloom that ate at her. Even though Tanner's Pride was the most handsome foal she had ever laid eyes on, Tanner's leaving made her spirits lower than a snake's belly.

She pitched fresh bedding into the stall as the foal hobbled here and there and suckled like a pro, even though he was only ten hours old. "Keep eating like that, Tanner, and you'll be one fine stud."

"Already am."

Charity turned and saw Tanner—the man, the very fine man—in the doorway. Gloom evaporated like steam off a hot cup of coffee. "Why aren't you in Alaska, or at least on your way?"

"Trying to get rid of me?"

She shook her head, not trusting her voice for a moment. Having him walk off was tough; having him do it twice in the same day was agony.

"I wanted to give you something before I left. Something for my namesake to enjoy." He nodded at the foal, then handed her a piece of paper.

"It's the deed for the fifty acres." She shut her eyes and opened them again and reread the paper. "What did you do to Billy Ray to get this? I can't even imagine what you could offer him. I tried money and..." She felt the blood drain out of her body. "Tell me you didn't do what I think you did."

"Hey, I tried to trade Puck, but Billy said Puck was too ugly."

"You traded your biplane. Billy always wanted it. Well, dammit, you can't do it. That's all there is to it. You've gone temporarily insane because you haven't had enough sleep. I'm going to Billy and getting the plane back."

She put down the pitchfork and made for the doorway as Tanner snagged her around the waist and hauled her back. "I can't use the plane in Alaska. So what's the point of me having it?"

Charity gazed into Tanner's deep dark eyes knowing she loved him beyond anything else on earth. No one took care of her the way he did or watched out for her or made her laugh the way he did or drove her to distraction the way he did. And he was leaving *again.* How many agains could she live through?

Losing him over and over was too much. She felt so tired, and Mama had Puck, and Savannah had Nathan, and Patience had chlorophyll, and Charity was losing the only man she'd ever love. She sat on the concrete floor and cried.

"*Oh no.* Don't do this, Charity." Tanner sat beside her. "Don't cry. I can't stand it when you cry. I didn't do this to make you cry. I did it because the land belongs to you. You worked so hard—harder than anyone I've ever known—and you made me find peace with my father and what happened between us and… *Please don't cry, Charity.*"

"Don't go." She handed him back the paper. "Take it, it's yours. I own a third of the farm, and I want to give you my part, this part. You can live here and live in Alaska and come and go as you want. No strings, no demands. Just don't walk out of my life and never see me again except at Christmas."

She swallowed and choked back more tears. "I love you. I want you in my life, but I don't want you to give up your dreams to be with me. There's no happiness in that."

TANNER FELT DAMN GLAD he was sitting. For the second time today she'd surprised the hell out of him—first with Tanner's Pride and now by giving him her land. "You can't do this, Charity." He held up the paper. "This is everything you've worked for."

"It's nothing without you. I'll just die here a lonely old woman if you don't come back once in a while."

"You're thirty-two. You're not eligible for Social Security just yet." He put the deed in her palm. "I left once because I couldn't see what life was really about, and I'm not making that mistake again. I'm staying. I love you, Charity."

She gasped in utter astonishment. "You…you do?"

"You accept me for who I am and you don't try to change me."

He kissed her gently, tenderly, tasting her tears, knowing he'd get to kiss her for the rest of his life and nothing—no adventure, no plane or flying—could make him happier. "Marry me."

"I can't. You'll die of boredom."

"Trust me, being with you is never boring. I can fly planes here. There're always emergencies of one kind or another, and I can fly people to remote fishing lakes and to hiking spots and to the caves."

He reached up and stroked the foal. "And I'll help you with this new little guy and maybe others. I'll sell the business in Alaska and we can build a house—"

"No, no. Don't do that." She kissed him to cut off his words. Then said, "Keep the business. It's part of you, just as the horses are part of me." She wiped away the tears and grinned. "I always wanted to see Alaska."

"As Mrs. Charity MacKay-Davenport?"

She threw her arms around him, toppling both of them back into the pile of hay. She laughed and kissed the dimple in his chin, then gazed into his wonderful brown eyes. "I can't imagine doing it any other way."

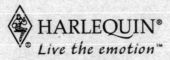

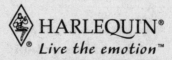

If you enjoyed what you just read,
then we've got an offer you can't resist!

Take 2 bestselling love stories FREE!

Plus get a FREE surprise gift!

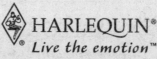